Billionaire Rake

MISHA BELL

♠ MOZAIKA PUBLICATIONS ♠

Published by Mozaika Publications, an imprint of Mozaika LLC.
www.mozaikallc.com

Cover by Najla Qamber Designs
www.najlaqamberdesigns.com

ISBN: 978-1-63142-846-3
Paperback ISBN: 978-1-63142-848-7

CHAPTER 1

Jane

"**W**hy not wait at the library?" Mom asks, and though we're talking on the phone, I can sense the worry on her kind face. "I thought this interview was important."

Important is an understatement. This librarian job is The One Ring, and I'm Gollum for it.

Gripping the phone tighter, I look around at my picturesque Central Park surroundings. "I knew sitting in the waiting room for too long would make me nervous, so I took a promenade." Not that it helped much.

Mom gasps audibly. "Is 'promenade' what the kids are calling Xanax these days?"

I almost drop my phone into the serene waters of the nearby lake. "A promenade is a leisurely walk in a public place. Sorry—another one of those historical romance words."

"Oh." Mom sounds way too relieved, considering

I've never done drugs. "Make sure to tell them how much you like those books."

Huh. Saying that I merely *like* historical romance is like saying Glenn Close's character was kind of into Michael Douglas in *Fatal Attraction*. Or that Hannibal Lecter was peckish for human livers with fava beans in *The Silence of the Lambs*.

The alarm on my phone goes off, spiking my heartbeat. "It's time to head over there," I tell Mom. "I only have ten minutes before my interview starts, and it's a five-minute walk."

"Go then," Mom says. "Hurry. I'm sure you'll crush it."

"Thanks." Hanging up, I smooth the skirt of the suit I bought with the last of my money—clothes I'll have to return if I don't get the job.

But I will, of course. This library has the best collection of historical romance in the world, and I'm the most avid historical romance reader there is. It's a match made in Victorian England.

Miss Miller tightens her stifling corset, readjusts her bonnet, and lifts her chin. During trying times such as this, a lady must keep a stiff upper lip.

Yes, that's better. When I need to calm down or cheer myself up, I often cast myself in the role of a nineteenth-century lady named Miss Jane Miller. She's the daughter of a baron who impregnated her mother out of wedlock and then promptly died on a ship that was hunting sperm whales. According to survivors, the good baron was humped to death by the majestic beast's eight-foot cock—which, to me, seems like a fittingly ironic fate for a useless sperm donor.

To further relax myself, I pop in my headphones and play the theme from Netflix's *Bridgerton*.

A menacing white shadow appears in the corner of my eye.

I turn, and my already-pounding heart nearly jumps out of my throat as I freeze on the spot, a dozen questions forming in my mind.

Is that a sheep? If so, what's it doing in Manhattan? Why is it running at me? Is it wagging its tail? Can you be killed by a—

Snapping out of my stupor, I attempt to move out of the ruminant's path, but it's too late. The massive thing is already upon me, standing on its hind devil-hooves and plopping its front ones on my shoulders with the force of Thor's hammer.

I fly backward.

The ground slams into me.

Air rushes out of my lungs, and it's a struggle to breathe.

There's thick liquid all around me.

Blood? Brains?

No, worse.

It's mud. Mud that probably saved me from an injury but has destroyed my hopes of looking presentable.

I suck in some air and thank God I'm not dead. As far as embarrassing ways to die go, getting killed by a sheep is up there with getting mauled by a hamster and licked to death by a kitten. The fact that I'd die a twenty-three-year-old virgin would just be the cherry on top of a multilayered shit-cake.

The sheep is right in my face now. Is it about to eat my eyelids? Or chew the glasses that, by some miracle, are still on my nose?

Nope. It licks my cheek.

Its breath smells like chicken and sweet potatoes.

What the hell?

Wait a second. This sheep's fur smells suspiciously like a wet dog. Almost as if—

"I'm so sorry," says the sheep in a deep, rich, smooth-as-melted-chocolate voice. "The leash slipped from my hands."

"You're a dog?" I ask the sheep, my mind still muddled.

"I'm not," it—or whoever—says. "I'm Adrian. The dog is Leo, and he sounds like this." The voice changes to sound an octave higher and sped up, like this person has eaten an overcaffeinated chipmunk. "You smell good. The mud is fun. I'm sorry I made you fall. Sometimes I forget I'm not a puppy anymore."

The dog that is not a sheep—Leo—moves out of my view, and I finally spot the speaker.

The sight evaporates whatever air I've reclaimed.

The man's—Adrian's—face is perfectly propor-tioned, with an aristocratic nose, a powerful chin, and silver-colored eyes that gleam roguishly. Yes, roguishly. With his broad shoulders and dark, windswept hair that extends past his ears, he could be copy-pasted onto a historical romance book cover; all they'd need to do is Photoshop in some period clothing.

Taken by the Duke, the title of said romance would read. Or *Marquess's Reluctant Bride. Thy Name is Earl. Baron's Virgin Mistress. Scoundrel Viscount's Wallflower—*

He kneels next to me.

Are my glasses fogging up, or my retinas? Such unadulterated handsomeness should come with a warning.

"Are you okay?" he asks.

Am I? I'm anxious, shaken, and much too turned on considering my predicament, but mostly, I feel like I'm forgetting something extremely important.

Then it hits me.

The interview! How could I forget about that, even for a moment? Do I have windmills in my head?

"I'm late," I announce and move to sit up.

Hell's bells. My arms flail, and chunks of mud fly in every direction—including toward Leo, who licks them eagerly, and Adrian, who takes it stoically.

"Are you sure you're ready to get up?" Adrian asks as he extends his hand to me.

"It doesn't matter if I'm ready." I grab his hand—and then nearly collapse back on the ground in a fit of the vapors.

His skin is hot like a raging furnace, and that heat permeates my body, melting everything in its wake.

Uh-oh. Miss Miller feels a yearning in her most secret place. A most unladylike tingle that—

"I don't think you've recovered yet," Adrian says as he helps me get to my feet. "Let's have you sit on that bench over there."

"Can't," I pant, pulling my hand out of his grasp before I combust. "Must run."

His expression hardens. "You could have a concussion."

"And whose fault is that?" I narrow my eyes at him. "I'm late for an interview. For my dream job. Can you stop getting in my way?"

"An interview?" He drags his gaze over me. "Looking like that?"

I glance down and wish I hadn't. "Oh, no. I'm dirtier than a pig."

"Pigs aren't actually dirty," Adrian says. "They use mud to cool off, and as sunscreen and bug repellent."

Miss Miller fights the urge to slap the scoundrel's high-cheekboned face.

"That's such a helpful lesson in husbandry, thanks." I step out of the mud. My knees are wobbly at first, but with each step, I'm feeling more and more like myself— just a much, much filthier version.

"Wait," he calls after me. "Let me at least help you."

I don't wait, but he catches up with me and grabs my elbow—like we're about to go for a stroll before teatime.

Once again, my treacherous body reacts to his touch with the most inappropriate intensity.

Sheesh. If by some miracle I get this job, I'll have to move Project Grand Deflowering to the top of my to-do list. Not getting any for so long has clearly turned me into a hormonal powder keg, ready to blow the first stranger I meet.

Miss Miller finds that last thought unseemly.

"Would they let you reschedule?" Adrian asks, still keeping a hold of my elbow.

"I doubt it," I say. "I wouldn't."

"It's just that I live right across the street," he says. "We could get your clothes laundered in an hour."

I blush like the maiden I am. "Are you trying to get me out of my clothes?"

His smile is cocky. "Do. Or do not. There is no try."

I free my arm from his. "Keep Yoda in your pants."

A total rake. I should've figured.

Speeding up, I leave him behind—for a second, anyway.

"Hold on." He catches up with me, Leo panting at his heels. "I meant the laundry offer."

"And *I* mean this: even if I weren't in a rush, the answer would be 'hell no.'"

He sighs. "Can I at least—"

"This is my destination," I say breathlessly as I halt next to the library. "It was not a pleasure meeting you."

He smiles wickedly. "The lack of pleasure was all mine."

When I enter the library, the smell of books cools my burning cheeks and calms me a bit, at least until people start looking at me pityingly.

"I'm here for the interview," I blurt to the guy at the counter.

"Mrs. Corsica is through there." He gestures at the door behind him. Wincing visibly, he adds, "She won't be pleased that you're late."

So on top of being inappropriately aroused and covered in dirt, I'm also late? What's next? Bird poop on my head, so I smell like how I look?

I sprint for the office door like I'm being chased by wild horses. As I knock, I try to get my frantic panting under control.

"Come in," a woman's voice says in a displeased tone that doesn't bode well.

I enter.

To say that Mrs. Corsica looks stern would be to greatly understate the case. With her formal attire, straight posture, and cold gray eyes, she reminds me of a wicked dowager duchess who's just met a heroine she considers to be far, far below the hero's station.

God. Even if I'd come on time and looking presentable, I'd be worried about my chances with an interviewer like this. As is, I might as well forget about the job.

"When did you think this interview was supposed to start?" Mrs. Corsica demands.

I turn so she can see the mud, then say, "There was an accident on my way here. I'm very sorry." I doubt it would help if I also told her, "A dog that belongs to a very hot guy pushed me down." That sounds like a less plausible version of "the dog ate my homework."

Nodding disapprovingly, Mrs. Corsica says, "Do you mind doing the interview standing? That guest chair is an antique."

"No problem," I say with faux cheerfulness. In reality, standing when an older woman is sitting seems rude, but what can I do? It's not like I have a shot at the job at this point, so my best bet is to treat this as a chance to practice my interview skills under extremely difficult conditions.

"Tell me why I should hire you," Mrs. Corsica says, and I can almost hear the unstated, "Not that anything you say at this point will convince me."

This is the hardest part of the interview process because I'm humble by nature, so selling myself is much harder for me than answering specific questions. Nevertheless, I launch into the spiel I've rehearsed in my head for a few years, one that highlights how organized and detail-oriented, how good with the latest library tech, and how amazing at research I am. As a coup de grâce, I tell her how much I love reading and how big of a dream it is for me to work with books.

The whole time, Mrs. Corsica's expression is so unreadable that I start to wonder if she abuses Botox, is a poker champion, or was replaced by a wax statue when I blinked.

"Your only focus is books?" she asks. "A curator needs to be knowledgeable about many different forms of media."

I explain that I stay up to speed on movies and TV

shows, and even challenge her to ask me about one if she wants.

She does, and I get lucky for the first time today. Her question is about *Sense and Sensibility*, which I've obviously seen and read, having been named after Jane Austen and the film being one of a small handful of historical romances.

She next asks me about my Master's thesis and work experience at Columbia University's library.

As I speak, I do my best not to shift from foot to foot and not to think about Adrian, both herculean tasks.

Eventually, Mrs. Corsica must feel that she's asked enough questions politeness dictates in a case when you have no desire to actually hire someone for the job—a bit like my conversation with my date the other day, after the man turned out to be at least twenty years older than he looked in his profile photo.

"Thank you," Mrs. Corsica says frostily. "You'll hear from us."

Translation: you'll get this job over my dead body. Get the hell out of here, and for the love of God, clean yourself up.

CHAPTER 2
Adrian

"The lack of pleasure was all mine?" I say to Leo with a headshake as soon as the mystery woman disappears into the library. "Do *you* understand what I meant?"

Leo cocks his head.

I'm smoother than that, and my idea of flirting is sniffing a bitch's butthole.

"Oh, well," I say. "Maybe I'll say something smarter when she comes back."

Leo lies down on the ground and looks at me skeptically.

I thought stalking was my thing, but whatever floats your two-legged boat.

"You got me into this in the first place," I tell him. "The least I can do is offer to buy her clothes to replace the ones *you* ruined."

Leo whines—which makes me feel like I've won the imaginary argument.

As we wait, I can't help but picture how I'd paint the mystery woman. Or make a statue of her using the laser welding techniques I've recently mastered.

A smile curves my lips. To some, she might seem either dorky or like a sexy librarian. They might think she's like the heroine in *She's All That*—pretty but needs to take off her glasses and have a makeover. I think she's reminiscent of the Mona Lisa, with a face as close to ideal as it comes, and her glasses expertly framing that perfection. In fact, I'd bet a million dollars that if I measured her face and divided its width by its length, the result would be the Golden Ratio. Same goes for her other proportions: the length of her ears would be exactly equal to that of her nose, the width of her eyes identical to the distance between them, not to mention—

My phone rings.

It's Bob, one of my army of lawyers who's an expert at destroying my good mood. He's the best at what he does, but he has an annoying habit of acting as though the upcoming hearing is the most important thing in *his* life, instead of mine. As if *he* found *me* so that he can help, not the other way around. Sometimes, I wonder if he believes all the bullshit his opponents are planning to say about me at said hearing—things that, unfortunately, a lot of people believe.

"Hi," Bob says. "Did you hear from the agency?"

I frown. "None of the candidates they provided are any good."

"Are you sure you're not being too picky?" Bob asks.

"Oh, am I?" I rattle out the problems with the candidates that include, but are not limited to: a DUI, a racist rant on social media, and restraining orders from three different men.

"Hmm," Bob says. "Maybe we should find a better agency?"

I scoff. "You think?"

"We've got to do this ASAP," he says. "The relationship has to have lasted a while to sound believable."

My jaw twitches. "Tell me something I don't know—and make it good news for a change."

"The judge we're most likely to get doesn't have much of a gender bias," Bob says.

"That's great," I say, and my heart squeezes with hope. Ever since I saw my baby girl at the hospital—or maybe even prior to that—I've been doing everything in my power to be able to be in her life, which requires getting joint custody. The truth is, I'd even consider marrying Sydney, her manipulative mother, but not until I've exhausted every other possible venue.

"I've also heard from the company that scrubs the internet," Bob says. "Their job is done. Just make sure not to give them any more work to do, and stay away from substances."

I blow out a breath. "I haven't touched mushrooms in a few months. LSD even longer. You don't need to keep bringing that up."

"Sorry," Bob says. "You know how important that part is."

Of course I do, and it's not Bob I'm angry at, but myself. I mentioned micro-dosing hallucinogens for creativity in some interviews a year back, and Bob has reason to believe the other side might use that to make a case that I have substance abuse issues. Now, should they go that route, they'll be disappointed when they try to get a hold of any proof of me having said that, and I also happen to be taking regular drug tests to prove I'm clean as the whistle of a referee with OCD.

"Anything else I should know?" I ask Bob.

He launches into the rundown, but I have to stop him before he's done because I spot the mystery woman coming out of the library.

Judging by her forlorn expression, things didn't go well at her interview, and if so, I owe her more than just a set of clothes.

"I'll call you later," I say to Bob and hang up.

The woman descends the stairs, lost in her thoughts. Then, when she spots us, she narrows her eyes to little specks of amber. "Are you stalking me?"

I gesture at Leo, and in "his" voice reply, "I messed up, so I'm making my human make amends."

She closes the distance between us and juts a finger at my chest. "As I already told you, I'm not going to your place."

"Right," I say in my normal voice. "But there's a clothing store nearby. How about I buy you a new outfit?"

She sighs. "Is that the fastest way to be rid of you?"

I nod, and Leo stands to his full height and wags his tail at her.

She smiles at the dog, and it's not a Mona Lisa smile

but a wide grin. "His fluffy face reminds me of someone," she says. "But I can't recall who."

"Oh, he gets that a lot," I deadpan. "He's got one of those faces, you know."

Her smile vanishes. "Where is this alleged store?"

I gesture toward Fifth Avenue. "Not far."

"Fine," she grumbles and starts walking.

I catch up, and as casually as I can, I ask, "What's your name?"

She stops. "That's not something I divulge to complete strangers."

I extend my hand. "Just to remind you, my name is Adrian. Adrian Westfield." I pull out my driver's license and hand it to her. "See? Now I'm not a complete stranger."

Frowning, she takes a picture of my license with her phone. "Now that's in my cloud," she says. "If you eat me, the cops will have some questions for you."

Eat her? The part of my anatomy that she dubbed Yoda feels a great disturbance in the force, as if millions of vaginas have suddenly cried out in ecstasy.

Judging by her blush, she must realize the double entendre.

When I take the license back, my fingers brush against hers, and it's like being hit with that Force lightning the evil Sith can shoot out of their hands. The energy flows right into Yoda—and unlike his movie namesake, my cock doesn't harmlessly absorb it. Instead, I feel like Yoda may explode.

"Jane," she says, and for some reason, her cheeks turn

an even more delicious shade of pink. "Jane Miller. My mother is a huge fan of *Pride and Prejudice.*"

As we resume the walk, I ask, "The book or the movie with Keira Knightley?"

"The book," Jane says curtly. "My mom couldn't have named me after that movie because it came out after I was already born."

"I'm not falling for that," I say to Leo conspiratorially. To Jane, I say, "I want to make it clear—I wasn't fishing to find out your age... Even if, by seeing my license, you already know that I'm twenty-seven."

"What a gentleman," she says with an audible eyeroll. "Since you're dying to know, I'm twenty-three. Also, before you ask, I'm a hundred and five pounds."

"I would never ask that." I wonder if I should tell her she weighs exactly as much as Leo.

"I'm also five feet and three inches," she continues. "Which makes my BMI nineteen and a half."

"Seriously, I don't need—"

"My cholesterol is one fifty," she continues. "I'm a Scorpio. My blood pressure is 115 over 75 most days. My shoe size is a five. Anything else you want to ask? If I have any moles? What my poop looks like on the Bristol stool scale?"

"I didn't ask any of that, and you know it." Though some of it will be pretty helpful if I make a life-sized statue of her—but I don't mention this bit because she might twist it into something only a cannibal would say.

"Are we close to the store?" she demands.

I point at a boutique across the street. "There."

She checks it out, then stops and shakes her head. "We can't go in there."

"Why not?"

She doesn't seem like the type to be blacklisted for shoplifting, unlike one of the candidates the agency sent me.

"They sell the most expensive clothes in Manhattan," she says. "They won't let your dog in, and they will snub me, like in that scene from *Pretty Woman*."

I grin. "If they do either, we'll shop elsewhere and then rub their noses in all the commission they missed out on, like Julia Roberts did."

For the first time, Jane smiles at me. "You've seen that movie?"

"I'm a movie fanatic," I say as we cross the street. "I've seen everything. What about you?"

"I'm more of a book reader." She pushes her specs higher up her cute nose. "Still, watching movies is something I do with my mom every chance I get, so I've seen many."

There's a pang in my chest. I'd give all my money to be able to watch a movie with my mom again, no matter how crappy.

"What kind of books do you like?" I ask before she somehow picks up on my thoughts and brings up something I wouldn't want to discuss.

Blushing once again, she enters the boutique instead of answering.

Before following, I look down at Leo. "You have to be on your best behavior in there."

Leo cocks his head.

What are the chances they'll have a cat who dares me to chase it? Or a squirrel? Or my tail?

Sighing, I pull out my wallet and make sure I have my Amex Black Card so I can flash it if it looks like we might get kicked out. Then I step inside—and bump into Jane, who seems to want to escape.

"Leaving so soon?" I ask.

"They don't have price tags on anything," she whispers loudly.

I wave to a nearby saleslady. Given the way her eyes widen, I suspect she knows who I am.

"There's been an accident," I say. "We need to replace Jane's outfit." I point at a couple of mannequins. "She'll try that on to start."

The sales team swarms Jane like fashionista locusts.

Before I know it, Jane walks out of the dressing room in an Italian skirt suit, looking so professional she could get any job she wants, be it a CEO, an investment banker, or a mortician.

This is when it hits me. Another place where she would look great wearing that suit is by my side at the hearing.

Leo looks up at me with a lolled tongue. No doubt he can hear my heartbeat speeding up.

Great idea. Now go and pee around her, or do whatever it is humans do to mark their territory.

The more I think about this, the more excited I get. Thus far, from what little I know about Jane Miller, she's light-years ahead of most of the candidates the agency has sent me.

What I like the most is that she has a wholesome girl-next-door vibe to her that would contrast nicely with Sydney's cold beauty.

Is she single? Straight? Not a smoker?

If yes to all three, this is it.

Jane Miller is going to be my wife.

CHAPTER 3

Jane

"How much is this?" I whisper to the blond saleswoman next to me, and it takes all my willpower not to complain about how annoying the lack of price tags really is.

I know Mom would chastise me for being thrifty even when someone else is paying, but I can't help it.

The woman names a number.

Gaping, I wait for her to chuckle and say that she's just made a joke.

She doesn't.

"I can't let him pay that," I hiss at her. "The clothes his dog got dirty are one-hundredth of this price."

"He won't care," she whispers confidently.

"How could you know that?" I ask, eyes narrowing.

Now she looks at *me* like I'm making a joke. "That's Adrian Westfield."

"How do you know him?"

Did he sleep with her? When it comes to rakes, that's the default assumption.

She furrows her perfectly trimmed eyebrows. "He's a billionaire and the most eligible bachelor in—"

I tune out the rest.

A billionaire.

The most eligible bachelor.

Now that she's said it, it seems like I should've seen it. There's just something ineffable about Adrian, something besides his out-of-this-world looks. If this were Victorian England, I would've guessed him to be a duke or some other member of the upper echelon of the ton, so it makes sense that he's a modern American equivalent. Add to that the fact that he's walking his dog so close to Billionaires' Row and buying me clothes at a place that seems to randomly add zeroes to prices, and it seems elementary.

"—don't you read any tabloids?" the saleswoman asks me, bringing me back to boutique reality.

I shake my head. "Why read tabloids when I can read books?"

She shrugs. "Do you want to try on anything else?"

I dart a glance at Adrian. "What's your least expensive suit?"

Even if he can afford this, I don't feel right accepting something that costs this much.

Miss Miller approves. A lavish gift from a gentleman is indelicate because it has the appearance of a bribe upon the lady's affections. If he insists on a gift, it should be something perishable, and thus not leave any obligation upon the receiver. Things like flowers are good, or fruits and vegetables—so long as they're not of an indiscreet shape, such as cucumbers.

"That *is* one of the cheapest suits we have," the saleslady says. "All I can do is show you another one that's in a similar price range."

Wow. The rich do live in their own little world.

I walk up to Adrian. "We have to go to another store."

"Why?" he asks. "You look amazing in that."

I bat my eyelashes at him. The phrase "flattery will get you everywhere" is about panties, isn't it?

Miss Miller considers the warmth in her loins a breach of etiquette.

"This is too much," I say. "I can't accept it."

He sighs. "I don't feel right about what happened to your clothes. You'd be doing me a favor by accepting."

Even though my resolve is wavering, I shake my head. "Your conscience will have to manage."

"How about dinner then?" he asks. "And a chance to launder your suit?"

Dinner involves perishable items, so it would be okay, even in Victorian times, right? And now that I know he's famous, I don't have to fear for my safety... as much.

Miss Miller thinks the safety of a lady's virtue is something she should very much worry about. An unchaperoned dinner is a lot more wicked than a lavish gift.

"Okay," I surprise myself by saying. "I'll go to dinner with you, but no laundry. For all I know, you might be a dirty-clothes-smelling pervert."

I bet the saleslady from earlier overheard that last comment, and it's taking all her willpower not to chime in—probably in his defense.

"Just dinner," he says. "Any preferences?"

I shrug. "I'm not too picky."

His eyes gleam with silver. "What do you think of sushi?"

"That could work," I say. Truth is, I'm actually excited about that choice. I've been craving sushi, but because my mom isn't a fan, I haven't eaten it in a while.

"There's a great place nearby," he says and names it, but it doesn't ring a bell. Nor would it, since my sushi restaurant of choice is near my house on Staten Island.

"And you're sure about the clothes?" he asks, looking me up and down appreciatively.

"Positive." My rags have dried by now, right?

"Can I at least get you a car to take you home?" he asks.

"Bad idea. Then you'd know where I live."

He frowns. "Won't I find that out when I pick you up for our dinner?"

"Not if I meet you at the place."

He looks down at Leo, as though asking for his help. "I don't like the idea of you walking around dirty."

I certainly feel dirty right now, but not in the way he means. "Fine. You can get me an Uber. Economy. Not a limo. Not a carriage with horses—or whatever else you probably have in mind."

He takes out his phone and presses the screen a few times. "Uber. Right. Heard great things about that app."

It doesn't surprise me that a billionaire has never used Uber. What is surprising is that he's walking his dog on his own. Shouldn't he have a fancy dog walker for that?

"The app needs your address for this to work," he says.

Hmm. He's got an annoyingly good point, so I tell him what my address is. "But I'm still meeting you at the restaurant."

"Fine, but let's at least exchange numbers."

"Smooth," I say, narrowing my eyes. "I guess you've left me little choice." I snatch the phone from his hands, text a smiley emoji to myself, and reply with:

This is Jane, the woman you strong-armed into dinner.

When he takes the phone back, he grins, which causes all sorts of flutters in the pit of my stomach.

Miss Miller would've slapped the rake's cheek before giving in.

I go to change, and when I put on the soiled clothing, bits of dried dirt chip away and land on the spotless fitting room floor.

Grr. I almost regret not accepting the gift.

When I come out, I spot Adrian pulling his credit card away from a reading device one of the saleswomen must have handed to him.

"What did you just buy?" I demand.

He turns to me. "The outfit you tried on."

"Why?" I squint at him disapprovingly. "It's not like I wore it long enough for you to enjoy sniffing." At least, I hope not.

His smirk is cocky. "There's always a chance you'll accept the gift after dinner."

I roll my eyes. "There's also a chance that a winning lottery ticket will fall on my head, but the probability of that is pretty low."

"We'll see," he says just as his phone makes a sound. After checking it, he says, "Your Uber is here."

Yep. A car pulls to the curb outside.

"Let me get the door," Adrian says, and before I can stop him, he plays the doorman, first letting me out of the boutique, then getting the car's door.

How dastardly. It's like he knows that enjoying gentlemanly gestures is Miss Miller's only vice.

"Thanks," I say, for some reason hesitant to enter the car.

He bends over, as if to take a bow, but stays there, with his lips only a very short distance from mine. "No problem," he murmurs.

I stare at those lips, my heartbeat quickening.

He gazes at mine.

Some otherworldly force seems to pull us toward each other. I can see the sensual curves of his lips, so roguish yet so strangely appealing, the silver striations in his eyes, the strong, aquiline line of his nose... Our lips are but a hair's width apart when there's a loud bark inside the boutique, followed by the sound of something big clattering to the floor.

"Fuck." Adrian straightens abruptly. "I shouldn't have left Leo in there alone."

My face burns and my heart pounds like the drums at

Waterloo as I take a shaky step back, then turn and stumble into the car. With an unsteady hand, I slam the door behind me and watch as Adrian rushes to the store to deal with the aftermath of whatever Leo's done.

The car pulls away as I drag in air, willing my frantic pulse to slow.

Did I imagine it, or did we almost kiss?

If we did, was it him kissing me or I him? Does it matter?

Miss Miller thinks it matters very much—as it is the difference between a proper lady and a woman of ill repute.

I lean back against the car seat and close my eyes.

I think I made a horrible mistake agreeing to this dinner.

CHAPTER 4
Adrian

Since Leo has created a mess, I buy some more clothes in Jane's size to pacify the saleswomen. I'm sure they'll come in handy later.

After that, I take Leo home, making dinner reservations and arranging a car for Jane as we go.

For lunch, we both eat the leftovers from my cooking experiments the other day—smoked melon with eel for me, chicken gizzards in peanut sauce for him. As I eat, I debate telling Bob about Jane but decide it might be premature. I need to find out more about her, which I will do at our upcoming dinner. Then again, since I almost kissed her, she might well flake on the dinner.

How stupid was that of me? Just as I've met someone who may be the perfect candidate to help me win custody of Piper, my Yoda may have ruined it within minutes.

The food sours in my stomach.

No, I can't think about that now. Must keep busy.

Leaving the dishes for my housekeeper, I head into my studio to compose some music. I come up with a few bass guitar riffs—something that could become a song for the metal band that I'm in. Then I write a jingle for a video I've created—one that might become an ad for one of the million companies I've inherited.

My mind is still wandering, still trying to get back to the Jane topic, so I get behind my computer to work on the children's story that I hope to read to Piper when she's old enough. For now, I'm just writing the rhymes because I'm still pondering how to best draw the illustrations.

Dammit. Jane is still sneaking into my thoughts.

I pick up a book on poker strategy. Nope. I go online and play a game of chess with a guy who claims to be a grandmaster, but since I beat him within the first hour, I'm skeptical that he's as highly ranked as he claims.

Also, my mind keeps returning to the dinner.

The good news is, there's no text from her flaking out.

Maybe I didn't freak her out too much.

Back to work. I review some investments, answer some emails, and interview a CEO candidate for one of my foundations. Then I work on a few more tunes and write a couple more rhymes before calling it quits.

As I often do at the end of what passes for my work day, I search inside myself to figure out what activity I felt the most affinity for and, as usual, come up blank.

True, the children's book is a labor of love, but that's

powered by my feelings for my baby girl. Without them, I'm not sure writing and illustrating would be my calling.

I sigh. Even though my father isn't around to criticize me anymore, I can easily picture his scowl and his biting words. "A jack of all trades but master of none" was the nicest version of his usual chastisement, with words like "unfocused" and "rudderless" not far behind.

And hey, he was right. I'm twenty-seven and still don't know what I want to do with my life.

How pathetic is that?

Leo walks up to me and pokes me with his wet nose.

Don't we have a sushi dinner to get ready for?

CHAPTER 5

Jane

"How was the interview?" Mom demands as soon as I step into our house.

I turn so she can see the state of my clothing. "It was a disaster."

"Tell me over lunch," she says, and I do, including the part about meeting Adrian.

As soon as I mention tabloids, she gets her phone out and starts searching.

I sigh. For a while now, Mom and I have been more like friends than mother-daughter—for better, and sometimes for worse. She's only thirty-nine, so she obviously had me when she was way too young, and because we're so close in age, we have problems that are pretty similar: dating, job searching, et cetera.

I've seen her be motherly to my younger sister, Mary, and I sometimes feel a little jealous.

"He's hot!" Mom exclaims.

I sigh. "Did you not hear the part where I didn't get the job?"

She waves that off. "You're brilliant. There will be another library. There's probably not going to be another scrumptious billionaire who will fall right into your lap."

I'm glad Mary isn't here for this pearl of maternal advice. "That library would've been perfect."

Mom narrows her eyes at me. "You weren't prickly toward Adrian, were you?"

"Prickly?" You bring a date home once, and now there are these insane accusations.

"You heard me," she says. "It's like you never grew out of the phase where you tease the boys that you like."

"I don't like him," I say with a confidence I don't really feel. "Nor did I ever tease boys I liked." It was more like I was too shy to speak with them at all.

"Sure, you don't like him," Mom says. "That's why you agreed to go to dinner with him."

I roll my eyes. "Am I too old to get emancipated from you?"

She tosses a bookmark at me. "Where is he taking you?"

I tell her.

Her eyes widen. "That famous Japanese chef's place?"

I nod, a suspicious feeling creeping into my stomach.

Mom searches on her phone for a few more seconds, then exclaims, "Their omakase costs fifty times what they charge for the all-you-can-eat buffet at our favorite sushi place."

"Show me," I demand.

Heavens. It's true. This is like the damned boutique all over again.

Miss Miller thinks the gentleman may expect something untoward after that kind of dinner.

I reach for my phone to send Adrian a text, but Mom snatches it out of my hands. "Don't you dare not go."

"But that's too much money," I say pleadingly.

She pulls the phone away when I try to grab at it. "He's a billionaire. It might cost him more money to waste his time coming up with a new place to take you."

Hmm. Does she have a point? I look it up on my phone and learn that some famous billionaires earn up to eight thousand dollars per minute, which, if true in Adrian's case, would make Mom right. Maybe the cost of this dinner isn't worth bugging him about. The suit might not have been either. Not that I will admit that to him.

The door slams shut downstairs, so we wait until Mary runs into the room, brimming with enthusiasm as always.

"Hi, sweetheart," Mom says. "Did your dad feed you already?"

Despite looking like my ten-year-old clone, Mary is my half-sister and has a dad who has chosen to stay in her life, unlike the sperm donor who spawned me.

"We had salads," Mary says. "I made sure he finished his."

That's Mary, the child who makes the adult eat his vegetables—and she does it with me and Mom as well.

"How was the interview?" Mary asks me.

I make a sad face.

"Oh, no," she says. "But that library would've been perfect for you."

"See?" I look at Mom pointedly. "That is what you were supposed to say."

Mom bristles. "It's not like they said you didn't get the job."

Mary narrows her eyes at me. "They didn't reject you? Why do you think you didn't get it?"

I explain how I was covered in mud, arrived late, and had to face an interviewer channeling Meryl Streep in *The Devil Wears Prada*.

"But didn't Anne Hathaway get the job in that movie?" Mary demands.

"She did," I say sheepishly.

My sister spreads her arms in a "I rest my case" gesture.

Mom grins proudly. "I've said it before, and I'll say it again: this kid will rule the world one day."

The alarm on my phone beeps.

"That's a reminder," I say. "I have to get ready for the silly dinner."

Mary looks from me to Mom and back again. "What dinner?"

"Jane has a date," Mom says conspiratorially.

Mary makes a face. Though in most things she's ten going on forty, she still thinks boys are yucky—and sometimes I wonder if she might just be wiser than Mom and me in that regard.

"Help me with her makeup?" Mom asks her.

My sister's eyes light up. "A makeover?"

"No makeovers," I say sternly. "But you can do a little makeup."

"Sure," Mom says and winks at Mary. "Just a little."

Yeah. Sure. They'll be satisfied with just a little—right after they also sell me the Verrazano Bridge.

CHAPTER 6

Adrian

I look sternly at my dog. "Buddy, there's no way you're going with me to the dinner."

He stares at me with his puppy eyes and squeezes out a whine.

But Jane smells so nice. Take me. Take me. Take me. Do I need to remind you that if it weren't for me, you wouldn't have met Jane in the first place?

"Tiffany is on her way to stay with you," I tell him, and that seems to make him feel better because he likes his former dog trainer—who's now his occasional dog sitter. "She'll take you on a walk. Anywhere you want."

Her timing impeccable, Tiffany shows up that very second, and I leave her and Leo as I go get ready for the dinner.

"I'm not sure when I'll be back," I tell Tiffany on my way out.

She shrugs. "I don't have any plans. When Leo crashes for the night, I'll just let myself out."

"You're the best," I tell her.

She grins. "You look so dapper. May I ask where you're going?"

"You may ask," I say. "But I'm pleading the fifth."

"Fair," she says. "Have fun."

When I get downstairs, my limo is already waiting for me.

I call Jennifer, who is in my rotation of drivers but is currently pretending to be an Uber driver. Per my instructions, she's rented an armored version of the Toyota Camry, so Jane should be none-the-wiser about how much safer her trip is compared to a random Uber ride.

"Hello," Jennifer says. After a pause, she adds, "No, you have the wrong number."

Okay. Great. That's code for "We're on the way and on time."

My chest feels like it's expanding, something that usually only happens after a good workout. I guess I'm eager to see Jane again, but strictly as the answer to the wife question, of course.

Romance isn't on my mind.

And it won't be until I have 50/50 custody of Piper.

CHAPTER 7

Jane

When I walk into the restaurant, I audibly gasp—and not because of the amazing décor, a combination of Japanese themes with modern art touches. Nor is it the mouthwatering aromas that take my breath away. It's not even the fact that the restaurant is completely empty, at peak dinner time.

No. It's the sight of Adrian dressed in a smart suit that is messing with my breathing. His hair is neatly combed and—

"Hi." He stands up from the only table in the middle of the large space and pulls out a chair for me. "You look amazing."

And just like that, I forgive Mom and Mary for all the earlier fussing. Almost.

"Have a seat," Adrian says. "Please."

He holds the chair until I go to sit, so I get a whiff of

his cologne— which has notes of wood, honey, and mandarin, plus something virile that's uniquely Adrian.

Knees feeling wobbly, I plop into the proffered seat, and as soon as he sits opposite me, I blurt, "Where are all the other patrons?"

Obviously, I've got an inkling.

"Itamae-san let me book the whole place," Adrian says, confirming my suspicions. "So we won't be bothered, if that was your concern."

"Oh, I wasn't worried about being bothered. I just can't even fathom how much it would cost to book a place with a reputation for having the most expensive food in Manhattan."

Crap. Was that an example of being what Mom called "prickly?"

Miss Miller considers that rebuke justified, even if talking about money is poor etiquette under normal circumstances.

"If it helps, I didn't book the place for your sake," Adrian says. "What I want to discuss with you is a private matter, and I do not spare any expense when it comes to said matter."

Miss Miller suspects this gentleman—a term used loosely—is going to make a dishonorable proposal.

"What did you want to talk about?" I feel a coldness in the pit of my stomach and have no idea why.

Adrian opens his mouth, but in that moment, an older gentleman comes over to our table, holding a cutting board that looks like an abstractionist painting made from the gifts of the sea.

"No soy sauce, please," he says with a heavy Japanese accent.

To my surprise, Adrian replies in Japanese, and they go back and forth amiably, until the chef—I assume— walks away, leaving us with his masterpiece.

"You know Japanese?" I ask.

Adrian shakes his head. "I only speak it. The hard part is mastering the kanji, which I haven't done yet."

"Sure, *that's* the hard part," I say with a grin. "Do you 'only speak' any other languages?"

He shrugs. "I'm fluent in Mandarin, thanks to Nanny Hua. I can get by in Hindi, thanks to a long trip to India. Same with Arabic and Russian. Apart from those, I can read but not speak Italian and have a working—"

"I don't believe any of that," I blurt.

He arches an eyebrow, then says something in each of the languages he's just mentioned—or so I assume.

With a huff, I take out my phone and pull up gazzetta.it. Nonna—a.k.a. my grandma—taught me a tiny bit of Italian, which is enough to navigate that news site and find an article without any pictures. I thrust the phone into Adrian's face. "If you can read Italian, what does that say?"

He glances at the page. "It's about a sex scandal their president got embroiled in."

Hmm. Since I don't trust my own meager Italian, I use Google Translate to check—and dang it, he's right. "Do languages come effortlessly to you, or did you have to study, like us regular mortals?"

He shrugs. "When I was a kid, my parents had me learn perfect pitch using the Eguchi Method—which was my first exposure to the Japanese language. But more importantly, perfect pitch helps you learn languages, especially the tonal ones."

"Wow." The closest I got to any musical training as a child was when Mom got me a whistle to blow in case of stranger danger. "Does perfect pitch mean you can tell what notes are in a song after hearing it?"

He nods. "A pretty helpful ability for a musician."

"Wait, you're a musician too?"

He grins. "I'm many, many things."

Cocky much? "Like what?" I take the chopsticks and grab a morsel from the glorious plate—but don't put it in my mouth just yet.

He grabs a piece of sushi of his own. "How much time do you have?"

"That many?" I ask, fighting the urge to be prickly. "How about you tell me the highlights. Say, talents you've utilized today?"

Grinning, he tells me about his day, and the more he talks, the more impressed I get.

"I didn't get a chance to paint today," he says at the end. "But I usually do that every day."

"You're a real Renaissance Man," I say, not joking in the slightest. I have to admit, this makes him even hotter. I pull myself together before I start drooling. "Do you have any examples of your art?"

"Here." He pulls out his phone and shows me a painting of the sushi chef we saw earlier—only here, the older man looks deeply immersed in thought, probably pondering how to make the best sushi in the world.

"Amazing," I say and finally stick the sushi piece into my mouth.

Without intending to, I moan in pleasure.

Adrian's eyes grow hooded. "Delicious, right?"

Blushing redder than the salmon on the table, I nod.

He sticks his own sushi into his mouth, and I'm not sure if he's mocking me, but he closes his eyes too and grunts in the exact way I'd imagine him to while coming.

Miss Miller cannot believe a proper lady would dare entertain such a thought.

"Try the golden eye snapper next," Adrian says when he opens his eyes, and then he gestures with his chopsticks at a piece identical to the one he just ate.

I do as he says, and this time, I control my moaning, but barely. This piece is light in taste, with a hint of sweetness and an ineffable deliciousness that means one of two things: the chef is using something like heroin for seasoning, or he's made a deal with the devil.

Speaking of such deals, I can't believe I forgot what Adrian said mere minutes ago—that he's summoned me here for some dastardly purpose.

The golden eye snapper suddenly tastes like straw—a crime against all that is sushi.

"What did you want to talk to me about?" I demand after I manage to swallow my mouthful. "Something private, you said?"

Adrian's expression turns serious, and he mindlessly snatches another culinary creation as he gathers his thoughts. "How much have you read about me?" he asks after he swallows a piece that he doesn't seem to enjoy either.

"Nothing. It didn't seem right." I *was* severely tempted, though.

"I see." His lips part—making me want to nibble on them. "I guess I'll have to be the one to tell you." He winces. "According to the tabloids, I've slept with everyone possessing two X chromosomes."

Miss Miller thinks the word "rake" would cover that much more succinctly.

"And you haven't?" I ask.

He blows out a breath. "I was never as bad as they make me out to be, and as of recently, I have actually been celibate—which has not stopped the stupid articles."

Hmm. "If this is about breaking your alleged celibacy—"

"No," he says emphatically. A bit too emphatically not to be insulting, if you ask me. "Sex wouldn't be part of the arrangement, I assure you."

I narrow my eyes. "What arrangement?"

He groans. "I'm fucking this up, aren't I?"

"I have no idea," I say pointedly. "I'm still in the dark as to what we're talking about."

"I have a daughter," he says.

Miss Miller begins to suspect that this gentleman is looking for a governess.

"She's still a baby," he continues. "Do you like babies?"

A silly grin spreads over my face. "I have a much younger sister, and ever since she was born, I've been obsessed with babies. Especially smelling them, cuddling them, and simply holding them."

"That's great." He pulls out his phone, swipes at it, and hands it to me.

"Wow," I gasp when I see the little girl in question. "That's one adorable kid. And I'm not just being polite. She could do baby formula commercials, or star in a *Look Who's Talking* reboot."

"Thank you." He beams with so much pride it tugs on something green in my fatherless heart and raises Adrian in my esteem. "So... based on your experience with your sister, are you good when it comes to taking care of babies?"

"I'm a pro." Should I mention that I'm overqualified to be a nanny—which is where this seems to be headed? Then again, a billionaire can afford to hire someone with a PhD in Nuclear Physics for that job. "I don't understand what your daughter has to do with your reputation as a rake," I can't help but say. "Unless you've decided to set a good example for her? But no. She's still too young to care about what you do. Unless... are you trying not to make more babies?"

That last bit makes him wince. "I wasn't trying to make babies when I *wasn't* celibate. Piper's mother—Sydney—told me she had an IUD. I also always used a condom."

He grabs a piece of sushi with some yellow fish on top and chews it rather angrily.

"Sounds like Piper is a miracle," I say softly. "I've got an IUD, and the doctor said it's ninety-nine-percent effective."

Adrian's eyes widen.

Crap. Was that too personal?

Miss Miller thinks that topic of conversation never belongs in polite company. Ever.

Blushing to boiled lobster levels, I finish with, "A condom is less safe, but those two combined should make it impossible to get pregnant." What I don't mention are my mom's reasons for getting me the IUD—to prevent me from ending up a teen mom like her. In Mom's defense, she's never said that having me ruined her life, but I think it's fair to say that the IUD heavily implied it.

The irony of me staying a virgin thus far isn't lost on me or my mom—but that also isn't something I'd share with Adrian.

Actually, if there were a way to do it delicately, Miss Miller would make sure the gentleman is aware of her intact virtue.

Adrian looks around the empty restaurant, then whispers, "Between us, I later learned that the IUD was a lie."

"She lied?" I gape at him, the enormity of what he said rattling my virginal brain.

"She did, and though I don't have any proof that she poked a hole in a condom, I hope you can see why I might suspect that as well."

"Why would she do that?" I ask incredulously.

"As it turned out in the aftermath, she wants us to be together," he says with a sigh. "But I hope you agree, that was not the way to go about it. Especially when we're such a poor match."

"I'm not sure what to think," I say. "Does she want your money?"

He shakes his head. "She's an heiress. I think she just likes how everyone would perceive her if she married me."

"I see," I say, though I don't. Not fully. "I still don't get what any of this has to do with me." Unless it's a nanny gig, in which case he's sharing way too much.

"Sydney wouldn't let me see Piper unless we got married," Adrian says. "I have since proven my paternity and can see Piper on a limited basis, but I want equal custody. I hope that's reasonable?"

"Sure," I say in the greatest understatement of all time. I would've given anything for the sperm donor who was my father to have wanted that. "I still don't see—"

"Her lawyers are going to do everything they can to make me look unsuitable at our upcoming hearing," he says. "My so-called 'promiscuous behavior' is something they are likely to use... which is where you'd come in."

"I'm still confused." Does he want me to teach him how to *not* sleep around? My qualifications being that I'm a virgin?

"If I were to get married—and look to the world to be blissfully in love—it would provide me with an air of stability," Adrian says.

No.

He can't mean it.

He sets his chopsticks down. "Judging by your expression, you've figured out what I'm after," he says, his voice brimming with concern. "And now there's disgust on your face."

I blush again. "It's not disgust. It's mortification."

His shoulders sag. "That's not much better."

"I'm not saying no... not that you've asked anything yet."

"Oh." He straightens, eyes gleaming with hope. "In that case, let me formally ask you." He gets out of his chair and goes down on one knee. "Jane Miller, will you do me the honor of pretending to marry me?"

Yep. I was right, but until he said the words, there was a possibility for a misunderstanding.

Now things are crystal clear.

I am to have a marriage of convenience... with a rake.

CHAPTER 8

Adrian

It's official. Emotions on Jane's face are harder to discern than those on the Mona Lisa's.

Suddenly feeling stupid about the knee, I get back into my chair and do my best to enjoy a piece of bluefin tuna as Jane gathers her thoughts.

"Look," she says, her chopsticks hovering just above an ahi piece. "I think it's admirable that you want to be in your daughter's life—"

"But?" I say with a sigh.

"But why would you want to marry *me*?" She closes the chopsticks over the piece of sushi and sets it on her plate. "Wouldn't some famous model be more realistic in such a role? Don't your kind of people have something like a marriage mart?"

Marriage mart? Sounds like Walmart's nuptial-obsessed brother.

"When I saw you wearing that suit at the boutique, I pictured you in the courtroom and thought you'd be perfect," I say earnestly. "There's something respectable about you. Something proper. Something that wouldn't scream 'she's just with him for his money.'"

"Thank you?" she says. "I think."

Did I put my foot in my mouth again? "It was totally a compliment," I reassure her. "You're the kind of woman I've never been with before, so selling people on the idea that I settled down with *you* should be easier than in the case of a model or an actress."

"Again, that doesn't fully sound like a compliment." She mindlessly separates the fish on her sushi from the rice, and I hope the chef doesn't see the sacrilege, or else he might just ban me.

"Again, I assure you," I say. "I mean it all as a compliment. I swear."

"Fine." She chews on her lip. "I don't mean to sound indelicate, given that your daughter's custody is on the line, to which I'm sympathetic and all, but... why would *I* fake-marry you?" she asks and finally sticks the ahi she's tortured into her mouth.

All right. Now we're on my turf. "You'll marry me because I'll pay you ten million dollars."

I thought people only did spit takes in movies, but she does a major one, the chewed-up fish dropping back onto her plate.

If the chef saw *that,* he might actually commit seppuku with his sharpest yanagiba.

"Sorry about that," she mumbles. She sticks the food back into her mouth and swallows it without chewing further. "You caught me off guard with that obscene number."

I shrug. "I know I'm asking you to do something crazy, something that would also take three years to resolve."

"Oh," she says.

"Yeah," I say. "Three years where you can't date."

"Oh." She grabs her water and takes a sip.

"Which is why, if you want to name a higher number, I'm okay with that."

I can see she almost does another spit take but stops herself in time. "That number will be sufficient," she says. "Assuming we agree on what you mean by 'pretending' in the context of this marriage."

Dare I hope she's considering this? "As I tried to say earlier, no intimacy would be involved," I say quickly. "Apart from, perhaps, some occasional PDA to create a digital trail."

Shit. She's blushing again. I probably should've left that PDA bit for later, after she says yes.

"We'd have to agree ahead of time on what we do or don't do," she says.

Whew. "Of course. I'm thinking we will have two contracts between us. A secret one, which will outline things like the PDA, and a standard prenup the world can know about, which will state that if we were to get divorced after three years of marriage, you'd walk away with ten million dollars. The reason for our divorce will be in our secret contract—something that would sound plausible, like, say, different values when it comes to parenting or something like that."

"And your custody will not change if we get divorced?" she asks.

I shake my head. "Once the child is used to being around me, the courts will not rock that boat. Bob—my lawyer—thought a couple of years should do the trick, but I decided to make it three just to be safe."

She blushes again. "And just to clarify... we can't date anyone in that time?"

Shit. "I'm so sorry. I totally forgot to ask if you're currently single. If you aren't and want to see a boyfriend on the side, that would actually be a problem, so if that's—"

"It's not that," she says. "The opposite, sort of."

I watch her face in confusion.

The color we call red is really electromagnetic radiation at a wavelength between 625 and 740 nanometers, and Jane's cheeks seem to traverse that whole spectrum before she says in a choked voice, "I'm twenty-three, and I've never gone all the way."

Wow. I'm speechless—apart from the extremely inappropriate solutions that are coming from Yoda, such as, "Fix the problem, I can."

"Fifteen million?" is the best I can come up with.

She doesn't seem to hear me. Cheeks going into infrared territory, she adds, "In three years, I'll be twenty-six—and I hope to have had my GD by then."

"I take it you're not talking about Gadolinium, the rare-earth element with the atomic number of sixty-four?" What? Why even bother talking when you say nonsense like that?

Jane blushes some more—which is an odd reaction to my chemistry trivia geekout. "GD stands for Grand Deflowering," she whispers. "Not letters in the periodic table."

Fuck me. Yoda is turning into the Hulk. "Twenty million?" I venture.

"I can't believe I just told you about my GD," Jane says. "I never talk about it with anyone. Ever."

"Look on the bright side," I say. "Talking about it just netted you ten extra million."

She shakes her head. "I can't accept that much money. Not when you're just being a good dad."

"I will not accept your help without properly compensating you," I say firmly. "Twenty million to me is like three months' salary for an average person."

"But it's a fortune to me," she says stubbornly.

"Which will make me feel better about depriving you of your GD for three more years, as well as the other unforeseen headaches this arrangement will bring."

She sits there, deep in thought, and mindlessly grabs a piece of sushi that has a piece of chinook salmon on top —which coincidentally matches the current shade of her ever-changing cheeks.

"Okay," she says when she's done swallowing.

"Okay... as in, yes to my proposal?"

She smiles weakly. "You're not going to take a knee again, are you?"

"I will if it helps." I stand up, ready to get into position.

"No need," she says.

I sit back down. Then, on a whim, I reach out, grab her slender hand, and hold it in the air in front of me as I solemnly say, "Jane Miller, will you do me the honor of becoming my wife?" This time, I remember to pull out the ring box from my left pocket, the one that contains the engagement ring my dad gave my mom twenty-eight years ago.

At the sight of the ring, Jane's eyes get misty, which sends a pang of guilt down my chest for putting an innocent woman through this. "Yes," she says in one gasp.

I slip the ring onto her finger—and in a sign from the universe, it fits perfectly, like it was custom made for Jane.

CHAPTER 9

Jane

I stare at my finger, stupefied.

I'm engaged.

Me.

To a billionaire.

Who's going to believe this? It's as plausible as a scullery maid getting engaged to a peer of the realm.

Miss Miller is suffering from palpitations.

"What do I tell people?" I ask, eyes still on the ring—which looks like something out of a fairytale.

"Great question," Adrian says. "We need to agree on our backstory and then stick to it."

I finally look up. "A story?"

He smirks. "As much as people think that I'm a catch, they might be suspicious if we tell them you agreed to marry me on the same day that we met."

"I'm not so sure about that," I say, my cheeks burning. "But the reverse is certainly not so plausible."

At best, a member of the ton makes someone like a maid his mistress, not his wife.

Adrian frowns. "You don't give yourself enough credit."

My chest feels light and fluttery. "Is this how rakes like you usually operate? No wonder it works."

"Did you just call me a tool?" he asks with a chuckle. "And a gardening tool at that?"

I scoff. "A rake is a term from historical novels. It's somewhat similar to a manwhore but with more style."

"Ah. In that case, my days as a rake are now over. Same goes for being a pruner, a trowel, a lopper, and a cultivator." In contrast to his words, he smiles rakishly and glides his hand through his long, dark hair, also rakishly. "Actually, I already knew what a rake is," he adds. "And you have to admit, a romance novel rake is usually a bit of a tool."

Yeah. Right. Of course he knew. "Back to the backstory." I grab my chopsticks and pick out a morsel from the giant sushi board, feeling proud that my hands aren't trembling... much.

"Right." He also picks up a sushi piece. "We met the way we met today—to make it easier to remember—but six months ago. Because of stupid tabloids, you wanted to date me in secret until you felt that I was truly reformed and things between us were serious. We're going to let people know about us now, though, since we've gotten engaged and you're about to move in with—"

"I what?" My chopsticks and sushi drop on my plate with a clank.

"Well, yeah," he says. "If we're getting married soon, it only makes sense to try to live together. I'm sorry, I'm assuming we're going to live at my place but—"

"It's not the location that's shocking," I say. "It's the fact that we're going to live under the same roof. That's pretty crazy."

He cocks his head. "You thought we'd be married but live apart?"

I blow out a breath. "I guess I didn't think that far ahead."

He looks at me worriedly. "Your compensation is still negotiable."

I grit my teeth. "Can you stop it with that? I'm not flaking on you, I'm just processing."

"I know it's a lot," he says. "But for what it's worth, my place is very nice, and the building has great amenities."

"A billionaire's lavish apartment is nice? What a shocker." I also can't believe that I refused to go over to his place earlier today, and now I'm moving there, sight unseen.

"You can come check it out today," he says, as if reading my mind. "Make sure *that* will not be a show-stopper."

I shake my head, but it doesn't make it feel any clearer. "You really think people will believe we're a couple?"

"Why not?" he asks. "We just need to do the necessary due diligence—learn all there is to know about each other and get the details of our 'secret courtship' sorted out."

"About that," I say, rubbing my temples. "Are you expecting me to lie to my family?"

Speaking of family... he may be insane enough to want to marry so far below his station, but his parents will probably have a fit.

He shrugs. "Do you think they'd buy it?"

"No way," I say. "My mom is my best friend, and we tell each other everything, even if I wish we didn't."

"That must be nice." His gaze turns distant. "We can tell her the truth then, but let me meet her first, see if she seems as trustworthy as you."

"What about your folks?" I ask.

The usual roguish gleam disappears from his silver eyes. "They died in an accident."

Oh, my God. How could I be so gauche? The signs were there, now that I think about it. What's worse is that I feel momentary relief about not having to face the disapproval of his crème de la crème parents, and that relief is followed by a surge of guilt that would kill a race horse. "I'm sorry."

"You didn't make my parents get on that fucking yacht," he says in a flat voice.

"Still, I'm so sorry that happened to you," I say again and cover his hand with mine on autopilot.

"Stop apologizing," he says firmly. "This is something you needed to know as part of learning about me. My parents have been gone for five years now. They had me pretty late in their lives, so I hypothetically knew that I'd lose them sooner than someone with younger parents, but I didn't expect it to happen like that, or so soon."

I gently stroke his hand. "You don't have to keep explaining right now."

He shakes his head. "I was an only child, same goes for my parents. Grandparents on both sides died of old age when I was too young to understand it. Piper is my only living relative."

My heart squeezes painfully. He's not just trying to be a good dad to Piper. He wants to have access to what remains of his family.

"I'm going to do whatever is necessary to help you get her," I say solemnly. "Anything at all."

CHAPTER 10

Adrian

It takes all my willpower not to do something stupid, like try to kiss Jane again. I blame the sadness I feel whenever I talk about my parents, and the softness of Jane's small, reassuring hand. Not to mention her heartfelt words.

But I'm glad I have self-control. Kissing her—or doing anything else along those lines—would undo everything I've accomplished here today. Every time I've dated someone, we broke up once the woman in question got to know me—and so it would be with Jane, but a breakup in this case would be a disaster.

Not to mention, I'm being presumptuous in my fantasies. Jane probably wouldn't even want me like that. The word "rake" wasn't a compliment, after all. And even if she likes me now, she'd lose interest in me once she learns how unfocused I am when it comes to having a plan for my life. In contrast to me, she was laser-focused on wanting to work at that library—which means that is something she clearly values.

In any case, I'm in no headspace to date anyone until the successful end of the saga with Piper, and especially not a woman who wants a Grand Deflowering. I can't be the guy for that. That honor belongs to someone she'll fall in love with and who'll love her back.

"Do you want to learn something about me?" Jane suggests, bringing me back to Earth.

"Please." I gently free my hand. "Let's talk about your family. So far you've mentioned your BFF mom and your much-younger sister."

"Right," she says. "I also have a grandmother, Mom's mom, who lives in Florida. My dad isn't in the picture at all, so I can't really tell you anything about him or that side of the family."

"I see." Should I add that I think her father is a moron?

"On the bright side, less lying," she says. "Mary, my sister, will believe we've been secretly dating, and so will Grandma. You can make my mom sign an NDA. She's terrified of lawyers and therefore will keep her mouth shut." She frowns. "I'm amazed you didn't make me sign one before you told me the whole plan."

"You seem trustworthy," I say with a wink. "Besides, I didn't think you would sign anything without an explanation. It was a miracle you didn't bolt when you saw the empty restaurant."

She grins. "It's not like anyone would believe me if I told them you wanted to marry me."

I sigh. "You keep not giving yourself enough credit."

She waves her ring finger. "I guess people will believe me once you tell everyone we're engaged."

"Okay, you win," I say. "Our secret contract will have a non-disclosure section."

"Thanks," she says sarcastically. "You should also threaten me with your fancy lawyers."

"To say my lawyers are sharks is to make them sound cuter and cuddlier than they actually are," I say with a straight face. "And don't get me started on Bob. He literally looks like a honey badger."

"Wonderful. Next, you'll tell me you can afford an assassin too."

"Why bother with that when my lawyers can make you wish for an assassin?"

She chuckles, but nervously, so I say, "I'll give you a million before any contracts are signed. That way, you can get your own shark lawyer to review everything."

She rolls her eyes. "You always go for the costliest solution, don't you?"

"No," I say. "I could've bought a private island for today's meal and had you flown there on a private jet that I'd also bought for the occasion. I did none of that."

"Oh, the restraint that must've taken," she says, hand clutching non-existent pearls.

Just as I open my mouth to make a retort, there's a thud on the restaurant doors, and when they open, Leo runs inside, his leash dangling behind him.

What the fuck?

Spotting me, Leo runs over and tries to get me to pet him—from under our table.

I'm so happy to see you. No, ecstatic. No, ardent. My tail actually hurts from all this wagging.

Shit.

The small table topsides, board crashing to the floor and sushi flying everywhere.

Jane leaps to her feet, no doubt worried she's going to be tackled again.

She didn't need to worry, however. When Leo spots the sushi, he forgets all about her and me and starts to feast as though he's been starving for a month.

"How did you get here?" I demand.

Leo looks up from his all-consuming task and tries to look innocent—a tricky proposition when your face is covered in rice and fish that you've just knocked over.

I was just passing by. Smelled you. Figured I'd say hi.

"Did you forget to feed him?" Jane asks.

"Of course, I fed him," I say. "So did his dog sitter, I'm sure."

In that moment, Itamae-san runs out of the kitchen, and the fury on his face reminds me of the menpō masks that the samurai wore to strike fear into the hearts of their enemies.

Upon seeing that expression, Leo stops eating, whines, and hides behind me.

I didn't do nothing. I was framed by a cat—hence all the fish.

"I've told you many times—you cannot bring a dog

to my restaurant," Itamae-san shouts in Japanese. "I don't care how rich you are!"

"I didn't bring him," I say. "He—"

"Shut up!" Itamae-san yells. "Take your beast and get out!"

CHAPTER 11

Jane

"We have to go," Adrian says to me after the chef stops shouting.

Feeling embarrassed even though none of this was my fault, I head for the exit—and smack into a woman who is gorgeous enough to be a model.

Spotting the woman, Adrian narrows his eyes. "You had one job: watch the dog."

This is his dog sitter? Does that mean she's around often? I'm not wondering this because I'm jealous. Just seems like something a wife-to-be should be aware of, right?

"I'm sorry," the model says. "This might've been a premeditated heist. He led me here and then ripped the leash out of my hand."

The chef yells something in an even angrier tone, so Adrian herds us all out. Once outside, he looks sternly at Leo. "This is my favorite sushi place. Now I'm probably banned."

Leo looks sheepish—or more sheepish than usual.

"I'm so sorry," the gorgeous woman says. "I—"

"Jane, meet Tiffany," Adrian says. "Tiffany, Jane is my fiancée—as of today." He looks at Tiffany pointedly.

Tiffany gasps. "This was your engagement dinner?"

I feel some sort of possessive satisfaction when I show her my ringed hand—which is silly, considering the engagement is fake and I have no idea if she has any designs on Adrian in the first place.

"I'm so sorry," she says. "Had I known, I wouldn't even have taken him for a walk."

Adrian sighs. "It's fine. Go home. I've got him from here."

"Am I fired?" she asks.

"No," Adrian says. "But you will hear me complain a lot if Itamae-san never lets me come back."

She smiles a dazzling smile. "Fair enough." Turning, she clickety-clacks away—leaving me to wonder why any sane person would walk a dog in high heels.

"So," Adrian says when we're alone. "That just happened."

"I know," I say. "Only a billionaire would get kicked out of the most expensive sushi place in the world."

Adrian looks back at the restaurant door longingly. "I might be forced to buy this building and then leverage that to convince Itamae-san to at least let me get takeout."

"I see a big problem in our relationship already," I say. "I have no idea if that there was a joke."

Adrian smirks and looks at Leo with a stern expression. "Are you going to be a good boy for the rest of the day?"

Leo looks back at his human with such guileless eyes you'd think it was the dog's evil twin—or some rogue sheep—that nearly destroyed the restaurant a second ago.

"I'll be good," Adrian/Leo says in that higher and sped-up voice. "And congratulations, Jane. When I smelled you this morning, I knew you and Adrian would be the perfect couple."

I cringe at the memory. "What kind of dog are you?" I ask Leo, then feel silly and turn to Adrian.

"I'm a Wolfoodle," replies "Leo."

I chuckle. "That can't be a real breed."

"My mother was an Irish Wolfhound," Leo says. "And my father a King Poodle—which is why I don't like the British and eat massive amounts of potatoes... au gratin."

"Ah," I say. "I thought cockapoo was the funniest-sounding mix. I was clearly wrong."

Miss Miller thinks words like "cockapoo" don't belong in a lady's mouth.

"You don't think Bossi-poo is worse?" Leo demands. "Or pomapoo, or peekapoo, or shihpoo, or sheepadoodle?"

"I think if anyone should be called a sheepadoodle, it should be Leo," I say. "Seeing how he looks just like a sheep."

"My favorite is doodleman," Adrian chimes in. "Which sounds like a superhero who can fight crime with his scribbles."

I grin. "Mine is huskypoo. Which sounds like something that happens when you're really, really constipated."

Miss Miller has just had a fit of the vapors.

Adrian's stomach growls.

My grin widens. "We should get something else to eat."

"Want to come over to my place?" Adrian asks. "I have some leftovers from a meal I made the other day."

"Sure," I shock myself by saying. "Let's go."

Miss Miller considers going to an unmarried gentleman's house unchaperoned the equivalent of taking a job at a brothel.

"I love NYC architecture." Adrian looks around with an excitement I'd expect to see on the face of a boy on a playground.

"You do? Why?"

"It's some of the best in the world," he says reverently. "Like that building." He points at the skyscraper to our left. "It was built soon after World War II and was the first time some of those techniques had been used."

"What techniques?"

He tells me, but I don't understand much, as what little I know about architecture I picked up when I read *The Fountainhead* by Ayn Rand back in school. Obviously, I was much more focused on the romance subplot of that book than on anything else.

Still, since he enjoys explaining, I nod and let him talk as I only listen with half an ear.

The feeling I'm trying to shake is that I'm going to a guy's house on our first date.

I mean, with my rational parts (the brain), I know this isn't a date, and that Adrian isn't just some guy. However, the rest of me (my loins?) still feels like we're on the way to my GD—which couldn't be further from the truth.

Hell's bells. Part of the reason I haven't lost my virginity is because I'm too smart to trust men, especially with my heart. That distrust goes double for rakes in general, but especially ones I find attractive, like Adrian. Rakes are where historical romance and reality diverge the most. In the novels, the reformed ones make the best husbands, but in the real world, they disappear from their daughters' lives, never to be heard from again.

"Sorry," Adrian says. "Am I boring you with all this architecture trivia?"

I shake my head. "No. It's actually interesting. Are you an architect yourself?"

"If by that, you mean someone who's designed a few buildings and made sure they were built, then yes," Adrian says. "If you mean someone who makes a living designing for builders all the time, then no."

"Languages, painting, music, ventriloquism"—I look down at Leo—"and now architecture. What else? Do you juggle in your spare time? Breed medicinal leeches? Milk snakes?"

He chuckles. "Is milking a snake a euphemism for something?"

Flooded by naughty images of Adrian fisting his

cock, I blush crimson. "Which is your favorite building?" I blurt to cover it up.

"The Seagram Building," he says without hesitation. "That is, if you didn't mean my own work."

I look around. "Where is it?"

"The Seagram? On Park Avenue," he says and pulls out his phone. "This is what it looks like."

"Ah," I say, not bothering to cover my disappointment. "I've seen it before. How is it different from other skyscrapers?"

He tells me, but once again, the architectural subtleties mostly go over my head.

"We're here," Adrian says when we approach a skyscraper that, in my opinion, is much more impressive than the picture he showed me. It has a steel framework that seems very masculine, though I'm sure there's a better architectural term for that. "I live in the penthouse at the top."

I whistle. "I thought this was a retail building, with offices and the like."

He shrugs. "It's that too. When I designed it, I—"

"Wait." I gape at him. "*You* designed this building?"

"I did." A wistful expression flits over his features. "It even earned a rare approval from my father. That is, until he learned that I'm *not* going to go on to become an architect, or open my own architectural firm."

There seems to be more there, but I'm reluctant to pry.

Leo pulls Adrian toward a shiny fire hydrant on the sidewalk near the building.

"Sure," Adrian says with a grin. To me, he explains, "I put that there for him."

Yep. Leo walks up to the hydrant, lifts his hind leg almost to my height, and does his business so proudly you'd think he was being knighted by the Queen.

"A sushi meal and then draining my snake." Adrian adds a large dose of contentedness to "Leo's" voice. "Now if I could just catch a squirrel and romance a poodle bitch, my life would be complete."

Miss Miller is mortified. Even this so-called gentleman's dog is a rake.

"Let's go," Adrian says and leads me into the lobby.

For some unknown reason, more than half of the security guards in this building are women—which I guess speaks favorably for whoever is in charge of hiring. That most of them are gorgeous is a little peculiar, and I'm sure I'm just being paranoid when I spot some of them ogling Adrian appreciatively.

"Hi," Adrian says to everyone. "This is Jane Miller. Please add her to the permanent approved visitors' list."

The tallest of the women types something into her computer while I stare at the artwork adorning the walls —paintings, statues, murals, and so on, each more beautiful than the last.

"Those are all works of Mr. Westfield," says the tall woman after she looks up from her computer.

I gape at Adrian.

He smirks. "Guilty as charged—and thanks to Susan, I didn't even have to brag about it."

"So you're a sculptor too?" I ask. "And a muralist?"

"I dabble," Adrian says with false modesty.

"Here." Susan hands me a swipe card. "We'll also need you to set a password." She turns her monitor so I can see, then slides her keyboard in front of me.

Pocketing the ID, I type in the password I've used everywhere since I was a teen: "MineTill12AM." It's based on my favorite novel, *Mine Till Midnight* by Lisa Kleypas, and therefore is not something I'm going to forget.

"That's not strong enough," Susan says when she spots what I wrote. "There shouldn't be any recognizable words in a password. There should be at least one special character, as well as—"

"How about this?" I replace each "i" in my password with an exclamation point—a trick I use whenever I'm forced to.

She frowns. "It's better, but—"

"What's this for, anyway?" I ask.

"My private elevator," Adrian chimes in. "The security team isn't here at night, but with that ID and the password, you can come and go whenever you want." Turning to Susan, he adds, "Whatever password she chose is fine. My apartment isn't exactly Fort Knox."

He puts his hand gently on my lower back and leads me toward the swipe thingy.

Rendered speechless by his touch, I swipe my new card and test my new password with trembling fingers, then let myself be herded into the posh elevator.

The doors slide shut, and I inhale the drugging scent of Adrian's wood, honey, and mandarin cologne—that is, until I also catch a hint of something barn-like. Wet sheep? It's coming from Leo.

"Want to see my studios?" Adrian asks, hovering his finger over the button for the second-highest floor. "Or should we go straight to the living quarters?" He moves his finger to the penthouse button.

"You're the starved one," I say. "You decide."

He presses the button for the studios—plural—and the elevator whooshes there with incredible speed.

"This is where I paint," Adrian says when we exit and turn a corner.

Yep. The giant loft is littered with brushes, easels, and other miscellaneous items I don't know the names of. An air purifier hums as it struggles to clean the air, but you can still smell paints, glue, and some other chemicals that must be part of the painting process.

In the next room is where he sculpts.

The one after that looks like a garage where a metal band practices.

"Can you play that?" I gesture at the bass guitar.

With a crooked smile, Adrian picks up the guitar and starts playing. It sounds good to my unfamiliar-with-this-music ears—like something from a Metallica album.

Miss Miller thinks this is exactly the kind of music that demons would enjoy as they frolic around in hell.

The next room is filled with classical musical instruments, of which I recognize the piano, the cello, the violin, and the oboe.

At my prompting, Adrian plays a tune on each one—

and if it were possible to have an orgasm from being impressed, I'm pretty much there now.

"What's back there?" I ask, pointing at an entrance we passed without him showing it to me.

"That's my private gallery," Adrian says and gestures for me to continue on a path that doesn't seem to include said gallery.

I narrow my eyes at him. "Are you a taxidermist too?"

"What?" He glances at Leo as though for answers.

I do my best to keep a straight face. "Do you keep stuffed women in the gallery? Perhaps the other dopes you lured here under the pretext of becoming your wife?"

Adrian chuckles humorlessly. "It's just a private gallery. Some of the pieces there are not meant to be seen by anyone but me. That is all."

"Right, right, right. But didn't Bluebeard also have a secret room the new wife wasn't supposed to enter?"

He sighs. "You agree to this being covered by the NDA agreement in the secret contract that you're going to sign?"

I nod eagerly.

"Turn off your phone," he orders.

"Hmm. If this were a Bluebeard situation, wouldn't he have me do that too?"

He rolls his eyes. "I think Bluebeard would sneak you into his building without alerting security."

I turn off my phone and follow as he leads me in.

The moment we clear the door, I gasp—but not because the room is full of tubs of blood, with the murdered corpses of his six prior wives hanging on hooks, as per the Bluebeard story. (Side note: wouldn't wife number seven have smelled the corpses?) No, my gasp is due to the works of art, each more remarkable than the last.

"They're not all mine," Adrian says when he catches me gaping at a suit of armor on display. "Some are pieces I got at auctions—for future inspiration."

"And that?" I point at a pyramid-shaped cloth structure attached to the ceiling.

"A parachute based on the design by Leonardo da Vinci," he says proudly. "It's made out of materials that were available in that day, and it actually works."

"Wow. Are you a fan of his because he was also a polymath?"

Adrian nods. "The more I learn about the man, the more I wish I could invent a time machine and go back to talk to him."

After what I've seen, if anyone were able to design and build one, it would be Adrian, that's for sure. "You'll have to tell me about him at some point," I say. "What little I know I learned from *The Da Vinci Code* by Dan Brown, which isn't exactly a textbook."

Adrian gestures into the distance. "I have a signed first edition of that book in my library—and every other book that mentions or depicts the great genius who was Leonardo da Vinci. Haven't read it yet, though."

"You should. It's fun—but lacking in romance."

Adrian steps closer to me, eyes gleaming. "What's your favorite book?"

As I tell him, my heart flutters from his proximity and the subject of conversation. "I also really like *More Than a Mistress* by Mary Balogh," I continue breathlessly. "As well as—"

"What about the books that the *Bridgerton* show is based on?" he murmurs. "The show is great, so I—"

"Wait," I gasp. "You've seen *Bridgerton*?"

This is what a Viagra overdose must feel like for a guy.

"Hasn't everyone who has Netflix?" he asks. "And how else would I know what a rake is?"

So he actually did know. I remove what little distance remains between us. "I *love* those books, and everything else Julia Quinn has written."

"Love, huh?" His lips curve temptingly. "That's a strong statement."

I don't answer. Whatever otherworldly force was pulling us together by the boutique is working its wiles on me once again. The sensual curves of his lips are like sirens, drawing me—

Something in my peripheral vision bursts the momentary bubble of lust—or whatever it was—like an ice bucket to the face.

That something is a naked statue that looks very familiar. Stepping out of Adrian's gravity field, I point at the statue accusingly. "Is that Susan, the tall security guard from downstairs?"

Adrian steps back from me, looking like he's coming out of a hypnotic trance. "I was just about to warn you."

Turning on my heel, I stride over to the statue and gape up at her face. Yep. It *is* Susan. The face and the height are an exact match, though I have no idea if her breasts are really this full and her nipples this hard, not to mention her—

"There's a reason I keep this gallery private," Adrian says.

Without answering, I scan my surroundings more carefully.

Oh, boy. On the wall south of us is a painting of a naked woman that I also recognize. It's Tiffany, the dog sitter from earlier—and she's just as nude as the security guard and with an even more perfect body.

"Do they know about this?" I demand.

Drawing or sculpting women naked without their permission feels like a violation—and if he's guilty of it, we're done.

Adrian draws back. "Who do you take me for? Of course they know. They gladly posed for me after I reassured them that I'd keep the final product here, never to be sold."

"They *gladly* posed for you... naked?"

He shrugs. "It's not like I hadn't seen them naked before that."

My eye begins to twitch. "Why did you see them naked?" A part of me can already guess, of course.

"I haven't hidden the fact that I slept around in the past," he says. "During that period of my life, the encounters were very rarely one-night stands. More often, they were short relationships, and some lasted long enough for them to want to pose for me—and that's what you're seeing."

My mind spinning, I take in the countless naked women in the paintings, and in a few instances, a couple of very attractive men.

"Most of these are professional models," Adrian says, following my gaze. "And before you ask, none of my flings were with men. I'm pretty much a zero on a Kinsey scale."

Since I'm still speechless, I just keep looking over the faces on display until I find another one that looks familiar.

"That's my Uber driver from earlier today," I declare. "How many women did you need to sleep with for such a coincidence to become possible?"

He finally looks guilty. "She's not actually an Uber driver. I didn't like the idea of some rando giving you a ride, so I asked one of my personal drivers to take you."

I face him, frowning. "She *also* works for you?"

He nods. "I've always tried to end things with women amicably, and we often stay friends. And when a friend needs a job and their skills fit something I need, I'm happy to help out."

I'm not sure if I want to smash my palms together in applause or across his cheeks. In a way, it's admirable that he's not a wham-bam-thank-you-ma'am type of manwhore. But on the other hand, this proves beyond a shadow of a doubt that he is a rake of epic proportions, and for whatever reason, my stomach feels distinctly unsettled at the thought of all those women still being in his orbit.

"Penny for your thoughts," Adrian says.

"Do you still sleep with any of them?" I blurt. And hey, still better than admitting that I want to burn every painting and knock down every sculpture with a mallet before possibly doing the same to the muses that inspired them.

"I told you, ever since Piper, I've been celibate," he says. "But even if that were not the case, I'd never sleep with anyone who works for me. Ever."

"You mean that?" I'm also wondering if he will consider me "working for him" once we're married—but I don't have the stones to clarify *that*.

"I wouldn't risk the custody hearing over some sex," he says.

Sure, but what about after that? I don't even bother asking this because the answer wouldn't be "I'll be celibate for three years." He's obviously going to get back to his rakish ways as soon as it is safe—but maybe be more discreet this time around.

Adrian's stomach growls again.

"Ah. Right. Let's go feed you," I say, glad for the distraction.

"You're sure?" he asks. "There's more stuff that—"

"I'm sure. The tour was starting to get boring anyway." A lie, but he doesn't need to know that.

With a sigh, he tells me to follow him and strides back toward the elevator.

CHAPTER 12
Adrian

How could I be so stupid? Why didn't I talk her out of going to the fucking gallery? Why make her face physical manifestations of my "manwhore" past?

Oh, well. It's too late now. I deserve the expression of disapproval on her face during this elevator ride. Even if she weren't a wholesome virgin, I should've avoided giving her such an awkward experience.

The elevator stops and Leo dashes inside, eager to play with his toys, no doubt.

"Kitchen first?" I ask Jane.

She nods. "I think I've had it with tours for the time being, nor do I want to hear your stomach make any more sounds."

Right. I take her to the kitchen, pull out the first thing that I see in the fridge, warm it, and set it on the table. All the while, the sullen silence on Jane's part reminds me of the mistake I made.

When I sit down, I catch Jane looking at her plate in confusion. "Is this crawfish?"

I shake my head. "It's langoustine."

"A what?"

"Also known as Norway lobster," I explain. "Unlike crawfish, it's a seawater crustacean—and you can taste the difference."

"And that?" She points at the other plate.

"Heart of palm panache," I say. "In case it's not obvious, I was dabbling with French cuisine."

Before my stomach annoys her again, I dig into my food and watch her do the same.

When she tastes the seafood, her eyes widen and another moan is clearly on her lips—causing Yoda to stir.

"Thoughts?" I ask.

She wrinkles her nose. "It's bland. And too chewy."

Yeah. Sure, it is. That's why she's wolfing it down like Leo does with peanut butter.

"Can we talk business for a second?" I say, figuring now is as good a time as any to broach unpleasant topics.

She spears the panache with unnecessary violence. "Why not?"

"I'll need to run a background check on you."

She rolls her eyes. "Go ahead, if you must."

That went as well as one could hope. "Do you want to take a preliminary look at the secret contract?"

"Dying to." She chews the panache with clear delight, but when she spots me looking at her, she wrinkles her nose and says, "You went overboard with the salt."

Should I tell her that I didn't even add salt? No. I extend my hand instead. "Give me your phone."

"Why?" Her amber eyes go slitty.

I resist the urge to sigh. "For security purposes—and to protect the trees—I never use printed contracts. I need your phone so I can install a special app for you. This way, I can use the same app on my phone to share legal documents with you."

What I don't add is that this is also the method I used to store the sexual consent forms that I always made sure to set up with the women in my previous relationships. Telling her that would be like the gallery all over again.

Jane takes her phone out but doesn't hand it over. "What's the app called?"

I tell her, and she informs me that she "can download apps with her lady fingers, thank you very much." Once she does, I explain that she'll need to give the app an email address that she actually checks and that she should memorize the password she'll use because resetting it is a pretty big headache—as I've learned from experience.

"Seriously, I'm not a nincompoop," she snaps. "In fact, one of the key responsibilities that I would've had at the library would've been to help people navigate technology—including reading apps that are not unlike this one."

This time, the sigh does escape my lips. "I'm sorry. I was trying to be helpful."

"There's a fine line between helpful and condescending," she says condescendingly. And weirdly adorably.

"I take it your interview didn't go well?" I ask to

distract myself from Yoda's continued demands for attention.

I probably should've asked this sooner, but her expression when she came out of the library spoke for itself.

I didn't think she could look more upset, but she turns out to be very good at it. "It was a disaster." She proceeds to give me the highlights, and I feel even worse now—and regret bringing up this topic so soon after my other faux pas.

"Is there anything I can do to help?" I ask. "I could donate money to the library, or—"

"You've done enough," she says sharply. "Plus, I only want to get the job based on merit."

I blow out a breath. "How about I send you the contract?"

She nods, so I do just that.

Jane reads the document over surprisingly quickly, considering all the legalese.

"Seems good at first glance," she says, looking up from her phone. "Obviously, the final word will be from my lawyers."

"Let me send you the prenup as well," I say. "And the NDA for your mom."

Again, she reviews it all quickly and doesn't think there's anything that raises red flags for her.

"Where should I send the money for your lawyer?" I ask.

She tells me, and I take care of it then and there.

When she confirms she's got it, I walk over to the

fridge. "Now on to more pleasant matters. How about dessert?"

She pushes her sparkling-clean plate away. "What do you have?"

"Parfait," I say. "Île flottante and my take on the macaron."

She puts a hand to her belly. "I'm not sure I have room."

I take out the parfait and two spoons. "Try this."

She gingerly spoons the custard-like concoction I made, but when she sticks it in her mouth, her eyes roll back in pleasure—making the situation with Yoda almost painful.

"How is it?" I ask as I eat a spoonful, doing my best to keep the huskiness out of my voice.

"Too much chocolate," she says. "And the strawberries must not have been fresh."

This time, I can't help but defend myself. "That's carob, not chocolate, and the strawberries were in a powdered form—made from freeze-dried strawberries that were the perfect freshness and ripeness at the moment of drying."

She shrugs. "Taste is very subjective."

"What kind of food *do* you like?" I ask, deciding not to push her further. "I figure that's something a husband should know about his wife."

I see her spoon approaching the parfait, but she stops herself. "It's a split between kedgeree, Yorkshire pudding, jam tarts, and crumpets."

I grin. "What they ate in Victorian England?"

She doesn't return my smile. "They're not *really* my favorites. In fact, I've never tried any of them. It's just a list I can spout off the top of my head, so if you memorize it, we'll be in sync if there's a test later."

I memorize the list and sigh. "I'll make your life even easier: my favorite food is sushi from the place we visited tonight—the one where I'm no longer welcome."

She cocks her head. "Your favorite is the most expensive place on Earth. Very relatable."

I push the parfait her way. "Do you mind finishing it? There's too little left to put back in the fridge."

"If I must." She demolishes the dessert and then looks at me expectantly. "Background check, contracts—do you have any other unpleasantries you want to get out of the way?"

"Not that I can think of," I say. "Would you like to see the rest of my home?"

She wrinkles her nose. "It's getting late."

"You are going to be moving in here," I remind her. "Plus, it's a good way to learn more about me."

"I've learned enough." She stands up. "Mom is expecting me."

Shit. I hope she's not pulling out. I walk her to the door. "Can I get you a ride?"

"No," she says vehemently. "I'll get my own Uber."

Fuck. This is about Jennifer's painting.

"In that case, text me when you get home."

"Fine." She does her best martyr impersonation and dashes into the elevator without so much as a goodbye.

With the sound of claws on granite floors, Leo walks up and pokes me with his wet nose.

Where's the lady who smells nice?

"She left," I say. "I really messed things up by showing her the gallery."

Leo wags his tail.

I think she'll be back. You can buy a lot of peanut butter for twenty million human dollars.

"I really hope so." Because if I fucked this up, I'll never forgive myself.

CHAPTER 13
Jane

W as it crazy to be rude to a guy who is offering me twenty million dollars?

I don't even know why I felt so annoyed with Adrian after the gallery fiasco. He warned me about his reputation, so I merely got a glimpse of how the sausage is made.

Heavens. Now I'm thinking about Adrian's sausage.

To get my mind on something else, I search for a lawyer—in case Adrian doesn't decide to cancel the whole deal, which he probably will.

Unlike some, Miss Miller is of the opinion that reformed rakes do indeed make the best husbands, and that this one can be brought up to snuff using rudimentary feminine wiles.

By the time I get back to Staten Island, I have a video appointment with a lawyer secured, and I've sent her all the prerequisite contracts. Once home, I slink to my room before I'm noticed and interrogated, so I can speak with said lawyer.

For a very stiff hourly rate, the lawyer explains what it is that I'll be signing, and her interpretation is pretty much the same as the impression I got when I skimmed the docs. In other words, I could've saved time by flushing that money down the toilet.

"Thanks," I tell her. "Sounds like I'm going to sign everything."

"No problem," she says. "And call me if you have any questions."

I hang up and go locate Mom, who's organizing the pantry for the umpteenth time.

"When did you get home?" she demands as soon as she spots me. "More importantly, how did the date go?"

It would be futile to tell her it wasn't a date.

"Where's Mary?" I scan the kitchen in case speaking of the little devil makes her appear.

"On her phone in her room," Mom says. "You can go ahead and tell me all the deets, no matter how X-rated." She grabs my hand and drags me over to the living room —which I don't mind so much because it happens to be reasonably far from Mary's room.

Once we're on the couch, I blow out a breath. "This has to stay between us. In fact, you'll need to sign a non-disclosure agreement before I can say a word."

"How very *Fifty Shades.*" Mom's eyes gleam excitedly. "I'll sign whatever you want if that means you'll dish."

I install the special app on her phone and send her

the NDA, which she signs on the spot. Then I tell her everything—or try to. When I get to the twenty million dollars, she looks like she's about to have a fit of the vapors.

"You're going to be rich!" she squeals right as I wonder if I should break out the smelling salts.

"And famous," I say with a frown. "Remember the tabloids?"

"Who cares? Can Mary and I live in your mansion?"

"What's wrong with this house?" I ask.

"The families of millionaires don't live in dwellings that are seven hundred and fifty square feet," she says firmly. "I don't make the rules."

"There may not be any millions," I say. "Let me tell you the rest of the story." I get to the part about the gallery, and how I dissed his outstanding culinary creations before cowardly running away.

"Oh, I wouldn't worry about that," Mom says. "He won't break the engagement simply because you got a little jealous."

I give Mom my best narrow-eyed stare. "I wasn't jealous."

"Oh?" She grins. "Then what would you call that green feeling of anxiety, anger, and confusion you felt when you saw one of his naked exes?"

"Can we rehearse what we'll tell Mary?" I ask, desperate to change the subject.

Mom looks at the door furtively. "We'll get as close to the truth as we can: you accidentally met the guy of your dreams. You didn't tell her right away, but now that he's proposed, you can't keep it a secret anymore."

"Guy of my dreams?"

Mom grins devilishly. "Like I said, trying to stay as close to the truth as we can. The lie will be the when—and not much else."

"Yeah, whatever," I say. "The key bit is that you knew about our relationship all this time, but we didn't tell Mary because he has a bad reputation, so I wanted to wait and see."

"Exactly," she says. "And I'll tell your grandmother that you got engaged to the guy I told her about."

"Excuse me?"

"Remember that idiot you dated for a week a few months back?" Mom asks. "The guy with the faux hawk?"

Wincing, I nod.

"I didn't have the heart to tell Mom that you retained your virginity."

"You what?!" I shout.

Miss Miller believes that merely thinking about matricide is a grave sin.

"Hey," Mom says. "I made our lives easier. You know how Grandma doesn't remember any names? Now we can just tell her it's been Adrian all along."

"Fine. I guess it cuts down on the lies."

"Exactly," Mom says. "Now go ahead and sign your documents too."

Oh, yeah. I do that—and a second later, my phone dings.

My heart leaps. "It's him."

Mom tries to snatch my phone from me. "If it's a dick pic, I call dibs."

I yank it out of her reach and check the message.

Looks like we're a go! Please give me a call when you're ready to plan the next steps.

"See?" Mom says. "He didn't back out—so call him."

"Tomorrow. Let me calm down a bit." Because I'm seriously having palpitations.

"Smart," Mom says. "For now, let's get Mary up to speed."

We head over to my sister's room, and I tell her what we've just discussed and show her the ring.

"I don't believe it," my sister says when I'm finished.

Crap.

"I know!" Mom says. "Our Jane and a gorgeous billionaire fiancé? But it's true."

"Not that," Mary says and turns to me. "I don't believe Mom could've kept a secret this big."

Damn. She's good.

"I held her first edition of *Pride and Prejudice* hostage," I say smugly.

In truth, I'm highly skeptical that the book in question, Mom's greatest possession, is truly a first edition. Mom never lets anyone touch it, but from afar, the book looks very old—and Grandma confirmed that it has been in our family for a couple generations. Still, a true first edition costs almost as much as a Porsche, so I figure Mom would have sold it long ago.

"Oh," Mary says. "That *would* do it. I guess congratulations are in order."

"Thanks." I ruffle her hair.

"Did you tell Grandma?" Mary asks.

"She knows about the boyfriend," Mom says. "But not that he proposed."

"Let's call her." Mary pulls out her phone and starts dialing before Mom or I can suggest doing so in the morning—because now is perilously close to Grandma's bedtime.

"Hello?" Grandma shouts so loudly her voice could reach New York from Florida even without a phone.

"Hi, Mom," Mom says.

"Georgiana, is that you?" Grandma shouts even louder.

Unlike everyone else in this century, Grandma uses an ancient landline phone, one without caller ID or even call waiting—a thing that has puzzled Mary, who's too young to know what a busy signal means.

"Mom, turn on your hearing aids, please."

Yep. She must've taken them out before bed.

"Mary?" Grandma says. "Jane?"

"I'm here too," I say.

"And me," Mary says.

"Hold on," Grandma says, and there's some sort of clattering, which hopefully indicates that she has in fact turned on said hearing aids.

"Can you hear me now?" Mom shouts.

"Why are you screaming?" Grandma demands. "I can hear perfectly well."

Right. And Adrian is a boy scout.

"We have some news," Mom says. "Remember Jane's boyfriend?"

"Jane's backbend?" Grandma asks.

"No, *boy*-friend," Mom enunciates.

"Can you even do a backbend?" Mary whispers.

"For Adrian, she might," Mom whispers back.

"Eww," Mary hisses. "Gross."

How the hell does a ten-year-old understand that joke?

"Ah," Grandma says. "Yes. The one who popped Jane's cherry?"

"Eww again," Mary whisper-hisses.

And how the hell does a ten-year-old already know what *that* means?

"Yeah, that one," Mom says. "He's Jane's fiancé now."

"He built Jane a fence?"

Is she just messing with us now?

Mom snatches the phone and puts it very close to her mouth. "They're getting married. He proposed *today*."

"Oh, goodness!" Grandma exclaims. "What a wonderful surprise! I guess sometimes they still do buy the cow, even after getting all that milk for free."

"Eww?" Mary whispers.

"I love being compared to a cow, Grandma, thanks," I say with an eyeroll. "Or is it milk?"

"Don't get snippy with me!" Grandma shouts. "Georgiana gave it away, and look what happened. Twice. You and Mary should know better."

Mom looks like she's been slapped, and I resist the urge to smash the phone into pieces. Grandma is usually kind, which makes it all the more shocking when she blurts shit like that out loud—especially since it's not even true in the case of Jack, Mary's father. He and Mom *did* get married, but then they got divorced in a year, so to paraphrase the horrid proverb, Jack bought the cow but returned her for a refund, regardless of all the milk.

"Well," Mom says, her voice exaggeratingly upbeat. "We'd better go. There are plans we need to make."

"Wait, when is the wedding?" Grandma demands.

"We just got engaged today," I say. "We haven't talked about the wedding date just yet."

"Good," Grandma says. "That means you're not knocked up."

Miss Miller thanks goodness two ladies are involved in this exchange, or else it would be pistols at dawn.

"Okay," Mom says. "Have a good night." And with that she hangs up.

Mary sighs and looks at Mom. "How long before you also go senile?"

I pinch her. "Grandma is not senile. She's uncouth."

"Don't say that," Mom says sternly. "Only I'm allowed to complain."

"Fine," Mary and I say sullenly in unison.

"Now," Mom says. "Let's celebrate Jane's engagement."

CHAPTER 14

Adrian

A video call notification shows up on my phone. It's Sydney, so I pick up immediately, as this is usually my chance to see Piper, even if it comes at the cost of interacting with her mother.

Piper appears on the screen first, and as usual, when I see my little girl, I feel my chest squeeze painfully and fill with joy, all at the same time. It's something about the little toes and fingers. And the chubby cheeks.

Sydney pulls her back and smiles, sapping the moment of some of the joy.

Seeing my ex-lover, I want to cringe, but I keep a friendly demeanor. Sydney inherited her Barbie-like looks from two generations of trophy wives, and on top of that, she takes care of herself with a vanity-driven obsession. She's lost all the baby weight quicker than anyone thought possible and is sporting what looks like lip injections, which probably explains why she hired a wet nurse the other week. Objectively speaking, she looks good. Unfortunately, she's too shallow to understand that it's not her physical appearance I find unmarriageable—it's the rest of her.

"Hi, Daddy," she says sweetly, voicing Piper in a mockery of what I do with Leo.

"Hi," I say, determined to stay cordial.

"About the visitation this weekend," she says. "I'm not sure if I can make it. Can we move it to Monday?"

My jaw ticks. "That's fine."

In reality, every moment of delay is like getting stabbed, but right now, I have to pick and choose my battles.

"Great," she says. "Are you going to The Ball?"

So this is the real reason for her calling. "I almost forgot about that, but yeah. I'll be there." Not that it will change anything. No matter how often Sydney contrives to be around me, it will not make me want to tie the knot with her. Quite the opposite, actually.

"It's a date then," she says, and before I can reply, she hangs up.

I blow out a weary breath.

If Jane pulls out, I'll need to find someone else to attend the event with me, or else Sydney will be even more sure that it's a date.

Leo walks into the room, wags his tail, and points his nose at the empty water bowl.

"Sorry." I pour him some water as my phone dings.

When I check the notification, my heartbeat skyrockets.

"She did it. She signed everything," I tell Leo excitedly.

He looks up from his water bowl, his whole face drenched, as usual.

See? You got this. Just sniff her butt very gentle-like when you see her next, and all will be forgiven and forgotten.

My elation lasts all through my evening walk in the park with Leo. Between Jane's acceptance and the successful completion of the internet scrubbing, I can dare to hope that the hearing might actually go my way, and I'll get to be in Piper's life.

Only one thing sours my mood. I can't shake the expression on Jane's face when she saw those stupid nudes in the gallery.

Hmm. If Jane had a negative reaction, so might someone else. A prudish judge, for example.

Shit. Could the gallery bite me in the ass?

Sydney doesn't know about the art, but many people do, so she or her lawyers could find out. Not to mention, Sydney has access to my building to make Piper's visitations easier, so she could theoretically stumble upon the gallery, recognize one of my subjects the way Jane did, take some pictures, and hand them to her lawyers.

Nope. I'm not taking any risks as far as Piper is concerned—not to mention, this way, Jane can come back to the gallery without getting upset.

Making a snap decision, I get in touch with a few people until I find out the most secure and private storage location for the art and arrange a move. In a few years, I might give the pieces back to the women who modeled for them, but for now, it's best they remain out of sight.

Still, even after doing that, I feel uneasy—because I don't think I've resolved what bothered Jane the most: the fact that my former lovers are working for me.

Could Sydney's lawyers use *that* against me? Twist things to make it seem like I slept with some of the women while they worked for me or in exchange for their jobs?

Nope. Can't take that chance either. In fact, I feel dumb for not thinking of this sooner.

Perching on a bench, I type out an email to Caroline and then call her. She's another person whose painting I'm going to be storing away, and she also happens to be the most talented headhunter in New York.

"I need you to find some people new jobs," I say. "Higher paying than what they've got now."

"Who?" Caroline asks.

"The links to their LinkedIn profiles are in your inbox," I say.

I wait until she reviews them all.

"A dog walker?" she exclaims. "You know I usually place C-level executives."

"I know your usual comp is a percentage of their salary, but I'll pay you directly for some of these more unusual placements," I say. "Oh, and I'll need you to find replacements for them—where, again, I'll pay a fee."

"What kind of a fee?" she asks.

"Name a number."

She does.

"I'll give you double that," I say. "And there's something else, for which I'll put a zero next to that number."

Her voice goes breathless. "What?"

"I'll need you to recommend me a headhunter," I say. "Ideally, someone as good as you."

"No one is as good as me," she says confidently. "But I can do my best... if you tell me why."

I explain about the hearing and how my former reputation might come up.

"Oh," Caroline says. "I'll say it again: Piper is one lucky girl."

"Thanks. You and I can still be friends, of course, and we might be able to resume working together in the future."

"I'll have my own firm by then," she says. "And I'll consider taking you on as a client—or not, depends on how charitable I feel."

"That's a deal," I say. "And I will recommend you to some people who'll keep you very busy in the meantime."

She thanks me and I hang up. I proceed to have a similar conversation with the folks who are about to find other employment, and everyone seems okay with it, except maybe Susan, whose husband also works for me.

"How about I find your husband and you a job together?" I offer.

"You think you can?" Susan asks.

"Of course."

That seems to pacify her, and I get back with Caroline to tell her she has one more candidate to add to the list.

Okay, I should feel calmer now, but I don't.

I guess the prospect of getting married—to Jane—is like a shot of espresso.

Speaking of Jane, once I get back home, I grab my Kindle and buy the first of the Bridgerton books in an effort to better understand my soon-to-be bride.

To my huge surprise, I get hooked on the novel and can't stop reading until it's finished. Wow. I really liked it, despite the fact that the target audience for this genre seems to be women, and that I knew what would happen since season one of the show was faithful to the book.

Well, pretty faithful. The book was more humorous, which is one of the reasons I prefer it over the show.

I end up buying the sequel but don't start it as it's already late. Instead, I shower and brush my teeth before jumping into bed.

Time for Yoda's daily Force training—or beating the bishop, as they probably called it in Victorian times.

Thanks to all the erections Jane has given me, this should go record fast.

Fuck.

I shouldn't think about Jane when I do this. I promised her things between us would be platonic, and this violates that promise, as do any fantasies where I violate her.

I empty my mind and just picture anonymous boobs and butts.

Nope.

The face they're attached to is Jane's.

Shit. I also realize that I might've lied to Jane when I said I was celibate. Does choking the chicken make you *not* celibate?

Whatever. Even my epistemological musings are related to Jane.

Must think of disembodied boobs. And butts.

I fail yet again because an image of Jane's oh-so-kissable lips invades my mind—and they are wrapped tightly around my cock.

And just like that, I come.

CHAPTER 15

Jane

I wake up groggy—and pretty certain I dreamed of Adrian painting me naked while I was covered in whipped cream. Or was it that he drew on me with whipped cream? No, I got it. He made a statue of me... out of marshmallows.

What could that possibly signify? I guess that depends on whether he ate the statue afterward or turned it into smores.

"Wake up!" Mary shouts and knocks on my door. "You've got to see this!"

"Go away!" I shout back.

"It's crazy," she says. "Come on."

"Fine." I get dressed and stumble out of my room.

"Living room," Mary says.

I let her lead me downstairs, where I greet Mom—and almost trip over a vase full of flowers.

Wait a second. There are vases with flowers everywhere: on the kitchen table, on the floor, even inside the microwave.

"What the hell?" I ask.

Mom beams at me. "Seems like now that your courtship isn't secret anymore, Adrian has sent you all the flowers he always meant to send you, in one shot."

Yeah. Turns out the living room is just the tip of the flower iceberg. Our whole driveway is littered with the stuff.

"Can you give some of these away to the neighbors?" I ask. "I don't think we can fit them indoors, even if we covered every inch of the space."

"Yeah," Mom says. "He must not realize how small our place is. But if you invited him here..."

There'd have to be an arctic chill in hell.

"I'm going to go brush my teeth," I announce. "If someone could free my chair and a plate's worth of space on the table, I would be much obliged."

I do as I said and wash my face as well.

Over breakfast, Mom peppers me with questions about Adrian, the answers to which I don't know.

Just as I'm finishing up, my phone rings.

"Is it him?" Mom demands.

I roll my eyes and pick up my phone as I head to my room and lock the door.

"Hi," Adrian says.

"Hi," I say, my spine tingling at the sound of his deep voice. "We just got the avalanche of flowers."

"Ah, good," Adrian says. "Do you like them?"

"There's *a lot* to like. How many flower shops did you empty?"

"What do you mean?" he asks.

I blow out a frustrated breath. "There are enough flowers here for two weddings and a funeral."

"Oh," he says. "I'm sorry if I got too many. I've never ordered flowers personally before. It's usually something my assistant handles."

"Sure. Sure. So you called the flower place and said 'give me a million flowers?'"

"No. I called, they asked if my budget would be as per usual, I asked if they could make something nice on that budget, and they assured me they could."

If by "nice," they meant "enough to invade my house with flowers," then they were telling the truth.

Cringing in anticipation, I ask, "What was the budget?"

"I don't think that would be classy for me to say."

"A thousand?" I ask. "Two? Three?"

"How much would be too much?" he asks, sounding sheepish.

"Oh, god, you spent *more* than that?"

"Five," he says. "But like I said, that's the standard budget when my assistant deals with the florist."

"Do they maybe provide flowers for weddings?" I ask pointedly.

"Usually, it's for fundraisers. Speaking of which, that's what I wanted to talk to you about."

"Fundraisers?" I ask, and realize he's changed the topic quite expertly.

"A fundraiser, singular. It's a big social event. They call it The Ball."

"Never heard of it." But it sounds fancy.

"Well, I'd like for you to go with me," he says formally. "It would be a great place for us to be seen together."

"I can't go to something called The Ball. I don't have anything to wear."

"That'll be easily remedied by a modiste," he says.

My eyes bulge. "How do you know that word?"

He chuckles. "*Bridgerton*. I read the book on a lark last night and have already bought the sequel."

What? Now I want to marry him for real, which isn't good.

"When is the event?" I ask, trying and failing not to sound breathy.

"Tomorrow. Sorry I didn't mention it earlier. I—"

"We only met yesterday," I say. "Don't sweat it."

Met yesterday. I can't believe it. It feels like I've been on this crazy ride with him for weeks.

"Does that mean you'll go?" he asks.

I bite my lip. "I'm not sure. I'd have to do makeup and hair, plus—"

"I'll have a team of professionals do all that for you. Say yes."

"Don't forget to invite him over," Mom shouts from behind the door.

Dammit. Was she eavesdropping this whole time?

"Did I hear someone say something about an invite?" Adrian asks.

"That was my mother," I say with an eyeroll. "I told her what's going on, so she's naturally curious about my fiancé. My sister is dying to meet you too."

"I'd love to stop by," Adrian says. "How about in an hour? I can help you deal with the overabundance of flowers."

My pulse picks up pace, and my face feels like it's about to catch on fire. "It's a bad idea."

"No, it's not!" Mom shouts from behind the door.

How did she overhear what Adrian said? Or did she guess?

I chew on the inside of my cheek. "If you come here, you might change your mind about marrying me."

"I won't," he says with great confidence.

"Fine. Come over," I say grudgingly. "But you've been warned."

Mom squeals from behind the door.

Miss Miller never thought she'd need to express this opinion, but squealing isn't ladylike, nor are any other sounds typically produced by farm animals.

"Can I bring Leo?" Adrian asks. "I don't have a sitter at the moment."

"What happened to Tiffany?" I ask, doing my best not to sound jealous and probably failing.

"Long story," he says. "The paintings and statues we discussed yesterday are now gone from the gallery, and their subjects have new employment. Hmm. I guess it's *not* such a long story."

"Why?" No way was it for me.

"I realized the artworks could be weaponized against

me at the hearing. And so could the fact that their subjects were working for me," he says. "I have you to thank for making me realize this and take steps."

As I figured, not for me. "You're welcome?"

"Seriously, thanks," he says.

"Don't mention it." The sooner I can forget about the women he's been with, the happier our "marriage" will be. "Take Leo and come over."

"Who is Leo?" Mom screams from behind the door.

"See you soon," Adrian says and hangs up.

I leave my room and give Mom a death glare. "Leo is his dog."

"Ah, great. When are they *both* coming?"

"In an hour." I mentally catalogue all my outfits, desperately trying to figure out what to wear.

Mom pales. "An hour? But the house is such a mess!"

Unbelievable. "Inviting him was your idea."

"Make yourself presentable," Mom orders and rushes away, issuing commands to Mary on the way.

I look into the bathroom mirror. Am I *not* presentable? Nope. Not compared to the women in the gallery.

Grr. I try on a few outfits until I like one enough, and then I do my makeup and hair as best I can—though I guess I could've asked Mom for help with the latter since she works in a barbershop. But no. Not while she's tidying up a storm.

By the time I deem myself presentable-ish, our front door dings, and I also get a text from Adrian:

Here.

I fly out of my room—and can't believe my eyes. Firstly, the flowers are now down to one big and beautiful bouquet, but more incomprehensibly, the place is spotless, the cleanest I've ever seen it.

"Who is it?" I hear Mom call from downstairs.

"Wait for me!" I shout and nearly fall down the stairs as I run down to join Mom and Mary.

"It's Adrian," he says from behind the door. "And Leo."

I open up.

Adrian blinds us all with his smile.

My mutinous heart skips a couple of beats as I take in his clean-shaven face, his silver eyes and—

"Hello, there," Mom says coquettishly. "I'm Georgiana, Jane's not-much-older sister."

Isn't the guy supposed to make that corny joke?

"Pleasure to meet you." Adrian takes Mom's hand and presses it to his lips.

Wow. Do I get the red-cheeks thing from Mom? Hers look like a female baboon's butt. When she's in heat. The baboon, that is.

Noticing Mom's reaction, Mary rolls her eyes so expertly I'm painfully reminded of the fact that she's on the cusp of becoming a teen, with all the angst and texting it might bring forth... unless she's like me, in which case it will entail lots of book reading and equal amounts of masturbation.

Hmm. Seems like my current life isn't all that different from my teenage years.

"And what's your name?" Adrian asks my little sister.

"Mary," she says, a bit shyly.

Clearly under the influence of the historical romance he's read, Adrian bows to her and pantomimes lifting a nonexistent hat. "Nice to meet you, Mary."

Now Mary blushes too—which is odd, considering her lack of interest in the males of our species. Even weirder is the worshipful expression on her face.

Someone might be rethinking the whole "boys are eww" paradigm.

"Let me also introduce Leo," Adrian says and steps aside to display his sheep-like companion, whose tail is imitating helicopter blades.

"Be good," Adrian says sternly and pulls Leo closer before he can knock over my mom.

"He's *so* cute," Mary squeals.

"Is she talking about the dog?" Mom whispers to me.

I don't know either.

"Come in." I gesture inside. "Please."

Adrian looks around. "Won't we get trampled by an avalanche of flowers?"

Mom's giggle is disturbing. "I called in a few favors with the neighbors," she croons. "And they took them."

This fast? Were they sexual favors?

"I owe you one," Adrian says and steps inside, pulling Leo behind him.

"Come to the kitchen," Mom says and leads our guests up the stairs.

Mary and I follow, with me appreciating Adrian's butt and Mary hopefully thinking about anything but that.

"This is for you." Adrian hands Mary a box of candy I didn't even notice him carrying.

Holding the box like a treasure, Mary mumbles a shy "thanks" under her breath—peculiar behavior from the most outgoing child on Earth.

"Did you make these?" I ask when the box is opened, revealing gorgeous chocolates. The box and the candy look too fancy to have been handmade, but with Adrian, you never know.

"No," he says. "These are To'ak chocolates. One of my favorites."

"I should make tea," Mom says. "Or coffee."

"I prefer coffee," Adrian says. "Thanks."

"Tea for me," I pipe up.

"I'll take coffee too," Mary says.

Mom and I look at her like she's grown coffee beans on her eyeballs. When she tasted coffee a year ago, she said, and I quote, "Why is everyone so obsessed with such a bitter and gross substance?"

As Mom brews the coffee and makes the tea, Mary sits at the kitchen table, sneaking peeks at Adrian when she thinks no one is watching.

It's official. She's got a crush. But does it have to be on my fiancé?

In Mary's defense, Adrian is a very crush-inducing man.

"Should I set out some candles?" Mary blurts.

"How romantic," Mom says. "Please do that, hon."

When Mary departs, I ask, "Should we feed Leo?"

Adrian looks at his furry friend with a grin. "He's eaten, but he'll never say no to more food."

I walk up to the fridge and scan for something that a dog would like before I spot it. "Peanut butter?"

Leo's ears perk up, but he stays with his back to us for some reason.

"Peanut butter is the elixir of the canine gods," Adrian says in "Leo's" voice.

I take the peanut butter out and spread it onto a paper plate.

"Here." I set the plate on the table next to Adrian. "Your dog, you give it to him."

"Ah, yes, my favorite treat delivered by my favorite human," Leo says excitedly.

Before Adrian gets the chance to place the plate on the floor, Mary walks back into the room holding the candles. She looks at the dog's snout with a shocked expression.

"That was Adrian speaking for Leo," I explain. "You're not hallucinating."

"That's not it," Mary says. "He's eating one of Mom's orchids."

By the time we all examine him, it's too late. The potted plant has been chewed and swallowed.

Wow. He even grazes like a sheep.

"Will he get sick?" Mom asks Adrian worriedly.

Pulling out his phone, Adrian asks, "What kind of orchid was that?"

"Moth," Mom says.

He does a quick search and exhales in relief. "It's safe

for both dogs and cats." Looking at Leo, he adds, "But you're still being a bad dog."

The look on Leo's face could be found in the dictionary under "innocent."

"I'll get you a replacement orchid," Adrian tells Mom.

"Just not a million," I chime in.

"No need," Mom says at the same time. "Thanks to your dog, Jane and you met. An orchid is a small price to pay for future grandchildren."

I was wondering how long before my family would make me want to fall through the floor. Turns out it took entire minutes.

Adrian's handsome face takes on a fond expression. "It's been months since our meeting, but I remember it like it was yesterday."

He's so good at lying. You'd think he were really talking about months ago, when in fact, it *was* yesterday that we met.

The kettle whistles.

Adrian goes back to his seat and starts checking something on his phone. Mary lights the candles over the stove, while I hand Mom the box with teabags and begin pouring water into the kettle—which takes forever thanks to our crappy water pipes.

A blur of white catches my attention, so I turn toward the table—and gape, as many things happen faster than I can blink.

Leo whooshes forward, clearly going after the plate

with peanut butter that we all forgot about during the orchid incident.

At the exact same time, Mary approaches Leo and Adrian, carrying the lit candle.

Oh, no! In his haste to execute the perfect heist, the dog bumps into Mary, which causes her to lose her footing just enough for the candle to come into contact with Adrian's hair.

Kill me now. The smell reminiscent of burned chicken tells me I didn't hallucinate what I just saw.

"Oh, my God!" Mary screams.

"Fuck!" Mom shouts.

Yep, all are very reasonable assessments of the situation.

Mind-bogglingly, despite having his hair on fire, the man is still lost in the oblivion of his phone.

"Adrian!" I pour all the water that made it into the kettle onto a gross rag that mom uses to save on paper towels. "You're on fire!"

Adrian finally pulls away from his phone, his eyes widening.

I cross the distance between us in one leap and smack his burning hair with the wet rag.

The fire seems to have stopped, but I smack Adrian with the wet rag one more time, just to be sure.

"Are you okay?" I ask Adrian, who looks stunned.

"I think so." He touches the spot that was just on fire. "What happened?"

I glare at the dog—who's devoured the peanut butter

already and is chewing on the paper plate itself. "Someone was being a bad dog."

"It was my fault," Mary says sheepishly. "I shouldn't have come so close to you with the candle."

"Hey," I say. "I was the one who tempted the dog with the peanut butter."

"It's okay," Adrian says. "I'm totally fine."

I bet this is another lie, just as expertly executed as the previous one. Yeah. It would've been ironic if, instead of his hair, his pants were on fire.

"I'm so sorry," Mary murmurs mournfully.

Swallowing the last bit of the plate, Leo finally picks up on the tension in the room and whines.

"I can fix this." Mom stands up straighter and examines the charred section of Adrian's hair the way Superman would a falling plane. "You'll just end up with a shorter hairdo."

Before anyone can so much as put in a word edgewise, Mom herds Adrian into the bathroom, makes him sit on the closed toilet seat, and pulls out her scissors and clippers.

"You might want to take off your shirt," Mom says. "Else your collar will be itchy."

Seriously? There's no way he—

Adrian unbuttons his shirt and takes it off like it's nothing.

Underneath, he has nothing on, of course, so my eyes feast on his hard muscular chest, his six pack, and his oh-so-lickable arms.

God help me. I might need a change of panties.

There's a gasp nearby.

Oh, crap. Mary is looking at the same droolworthy muscles as I am.

"Go watch the dog," I say to her, and then I position my body in the doorway to block her view. A ten-year-old is much too innocent to be exposed to something like this. She'll be ruined for all other men.

Heavens. Miss Miller feels a scandalous womanly condensation in the part of her anatomy that an unmarried lady shouldn't even think about.

Mom starts turns on the clippers, and the buzzing noise dampens my libido... a little.

"This reminds me of that horrible scene in *Thor: Ragnarok*," Mary whispers from behind me. "When they cut Chris Hemsworth's hair with a device that looked like the blades of a blender."

I ignore Mary because I'm annoyed at how close Mom is getting to my fake fiancé. Relatedly, does she *need* to put her boobs in his face when trimming the top of his head? Why is she even cutting that? The burned hair was in the back.

Whatever.

After fifteen minutes that feel like a month, Mom's hair buzzer stops.

"Have a look," she says.

I know she's talking to Adrian, but I'm only human, so I check him out—and blow out an annoyed breath.

If someone burned and then cut *my* hair, I would surely look hideous. But for Adrian, his already-sharp cheekbones now look like they could cut steel, and the angularness of his face has become more angular some-how, daring my fingertips to trace over his features and my tongue to—

"Great, thanks," Adrian says with merely a glance at himself in the mirror.

"That's it?" I demand. "You won't even bother asking for another mirror so you can see how it looks from behind?"

It looks amazing, of course, but he doesn't know that.

"I trust Georgiana." Adrian gestures at the nearby shower. "Do you mind if I wash the hair off?"

"Of course not," Mom says breathily but doesn't move. Nor do I.

After waiting for a couple of beats, Adrian smirks. "I might need a bit more privacy, if you don't mind."

Cheeks red, Mom thrusts a big towel into his hands and rushes out of the bathroom, almost trampling me.

There's the click-clack of Adrian locking the door, which is good, because when the shower starts, I feel very tempted to go inside—in case he needs some help getting soap on his back, of course.

"How does it look?" Mary asks us with the same intonation she uses when asking things like, "Do you think global nuclear disarmament will happen in my lifetime?"

"How about we wait at the table?" I suggest.

She and Mom both nod and we take our seats. The tea and coffee have cooled by now, so Mom warms them in the microwave. Finally, the bathroom door opens, and

Adrian joins us, smelling fresh and looking like his haircut cost a grand.

"Thanks again, Georgiana," he says as he sits down. "Between the new look and my beautiful fiancée, everyone at The Ball will be dying of jealousy."

Help! I'm a melted puddle, and I can't get up.

CHAPTER 16
Adrian

J ane reaches for one of the chocolates, and I do my best not to ogle her when she puts it into her mouth. There's a child present, so I need Yoda on his best behavior.

Jane moans in pleasure.

Damn it. How can I be *this* turned on so soon after having my hair set on fire?

Seeing Jane's reaction, Georgiana and Mary exchange glances and each snatch a piece of chocolate.

"This is amazing," Georgiana says after she tries hers. "Better than s"—she glances at Mary—"eafood."

"Seafood?" Mary exclaims. "It's better even than the smell of old books."

"Hey now." Jane grabs another piece of chocolate. "It's good, but not old-book-smell good." She channels Leo in front of peanut butter as she stuffs the next bit of chocolate into her mouth and then moans again.

Yoda suffers in silence.

"This chocolate was made from Nacional—a rare cocoa bean variety," I say, desperate to get my mind on something besides Jane's sounds of pleasure. "It was aged for many years in a wooden cask—hence the subtle notes you're probably tasting."

Jane stops herself from grabbing another piece. "Are you trying to get us hooked on a super-expensive chocolate, like some kind of drug dealer?"

Shrugging, I take a piece. "I don't like dealing with options, so when something is considered the best, I go for that."

"Right," Jane says with a slight eyeroll. "We wouldn't expect you to lower yourself to eat a Hershey's bar."

I wink at her. "I'd go for one of those Hershey's Kisses."

Her mom says, "Aww," and Jane's blush is back with a red vengeance.

Mary takes a sip of her coffee and winces the way I did back in the day when Mom used to make me drink fish oil. "How come this is the first time Jane has tried your favorite chocolate?" she asks after she's done grimacing.

Shit. This is an example of the type of thing that could trip us up at the hearing.

"He's a health nut," Jane says. "That's why he eats chocolate very rarely—and I didn't want to tease him by eating it myself."

Oh, yeah? "And don't forget—Jane is a reasonable-price nut," I say pointedly. "Which is why I've been looking for a subtle way to sneak this 'overpriced' chocolate under her radar—and I clearly failed."

"The word you're looking for is 'cheap,'" Georgiana says with a grin.

"I'm not cheap," Jane huffs. "I'm thrifty—which I learned from you, Mrs. Use-that-rag-instead-of-paper-towels."

"That's for protecting the trees," Georgiana says defensively. "If I were ever frugal, it was out of necessity."

Said necessity is over with, now that I'm in their lives—even if Jane were not going to marry me—but I don't say that out loud.

Mary's eyes are still narrowed in suspicion. "What was your weirdest date like?"

Fuck. This is a test. Must think on my feet, pretend that this is the hearing.

"We went to a cat funeral on our second date," I blurt. "He belonged to the CEO of one of my companies, so I had to show my support."

That was bad, but hey, now I have something prepared in case they ask this at the hearing.

"Oh, yeah," Jane says. "It was that evil cat."

Mary's eyes turn into slits. "If the cat was dead, how do you know he was evil?"

I think I might be a better liar than Jane.

Jane shrugs. "I simply assume. His name was Purrtin."

Or maybe she's not so bad after all, even if I would've gone for something like Kitler.

"That's pretty weird," Mary says, and her suspicion seems to ease. "Did anything funny happen during any of your dates?"

"Jane was attacked by a swan," I say. "But I protected her."

"What kind of swan?" Mary asks.

"Whooper," I say. "I remember because I made a joke about it becoming swan burgers, but Jane didn't get it."

"Oh, I got it," Jane says sardonically. "You forgot to mention you protected me by letting the swan bite your ass."

I chuckle. "And Jane was upset over how expensive the ruined jeans were."

Jane frowns at me. "Maybe we should tell everyone how you got bitten by a cow when we went to a petting zoo?"

Touché. "Maybe I should tell everyone about the time you dressed as an inflatable unicorn on Halloween, just to have the costume pop, like a balloon?"

"At least I've never gone to the bathroom in a poison ivy bush," Jane says.

And that's an image that quells Yoda's stirrings pretty effectively—unless... did she mean that it was my butt that made contact with the imaginary poison ivy? We'll need to iron out such details ASAP.

Suddenly, Mary squeals like, well, a little girl. Turning around, she blows out a breath. "It was the dog again," she says. "His wet nose touched my skin."

"He's begging for chocolate," I explain. "But don't give him any. It's toxic for dogs. Also, grapes are toxic—as are their shriveled by-blows, raisins, but he begs for all of those too."

"Here." Jane grabs the peanut butter from earlier, sticks her finger into the jar, and then extends it toward Leo.

The treat is gone in a millisecond, and Leo licks his chops with satisfaction.

"You might be my favorite human now," I say in his voice. "It's just as well you're marrying my former favorite."

Mom grins at Leo. "Once they have a baby, *that* should be your favorite human."

"Mom!" Jane says sternly and turns a delicious shade of crimson. "We're not even married yet."

Hmm. A baby with Jane. I'm not sure how I feel about that joke—but I do know I'd rather Jane didn't act as though it would be the end of civilization as we know it.

"Can you stop saying gross things so that we can get back to their stories?" Mary says to Georgiana petulantly. Turning to me, she asks, "What's the fanciest restaurant you've ever taken Jane to?"

This one is easy, so Jane and I take turns telling them about last night's sushi experience and how we're now banned from the place.

Mary's interrogation—I mean, friendly questions —continue.

She demands to know ever more obscure details of our imaginary courtship, and we make it up as we go.

Jane seems a little annoyed as she replies to her little sister, but I'm grateful. Thanks to this, no one will be able to stump us in the same way. The crazy stories we make up are very memorable.

I'm in the middle of the story of how Jane got stuck in a washing machine at my place during a game of hide-and-seek gone wrong when I get a text.

"Ah," I say, looking up from the phone. "Jane's modiste is on her way to my place."

Mary cocks her head. "Does that mean you have to go?"

"Sorry," I say.

Mary sighs. "You'll just have to come back. I have so many more questions."

She does? At this point, the only thing she doesn't know is my social security number, my cholesterol levels, and the position of Mercury when Jane and I had our first (and rather fictional) kiss.

"Maybe he will come back, maybe he won't," Jane says. "You can always ask *me* all the questions."

Mary rolls her eyes. "You'll only tell me the stories that make you look good."

Jane gives me a suffering look that seems to say, "See what I have to deal with?"

Georgiana leaps to her feet. "Thank you so much for coming to meet us."

"The pleasure was mine." I catch Leo, attach his leash back to his collar, and ask Jane, "How long do you need to get ready?"

"I can go now," Jane says. "Especially considering that I'll be getting a new outfit."

Georgiana and Mary pepper us with questions about tonight's event all the way down the staircase and as we walk to the limo.

When we pull away, finally by ourselves, Jane says, "I'm sorry about all that."

"I'm not. I loved your family." It's true—and not just because I have none of my own. They clearly love each other dearly and enjoy each other's presence, which wasn't the case in my family even while my parents were alive.

Jane puts a hand on my thigh. "How long has it been... since the accident?"

"Am I that transparent?" I ask, grimacing.

"You don't have to tell me if it's too private," she says.

I sigh. "If we're to be married, you should know stuff like this. I just hate talking about it."

She squeezes my thigh. "I'm sorry I brought it up."

"No. I'm glad you did. It's been five years. I still miss them terribly, but I feel guilty because I miss Mom much more. Dad and I had a complex relationship."

Then again, is it complex when you're someone's disappointment, or is it tragically simple? In contrast to Dad, Mom was proud of all the different things I was interested in, without needing me to become a master of any one trade.

"Nothing to feel guilty about," Jane says softly. "I

don't even know my dad, so I only care about what happens to my mom."

I force a smile—albeit a weak one. "Between this and your sister's questions, I think we can pass for having dated for six months."

She pulls her hand away. "I know, right? We just need to rehearse all the stuff we made up for Mary, and we'll be golden."

We do just that for the rest of the ride.

When we get to my building, I watch Jane's expression as we pass by security because even though Susan is gone, there are a number of attractive women working the desk still, ones I've never had any relations with.

Hmm. Blushing aside, Jane would make a great poker player. Her thoughts are unreadable as we head to my place.

When we step out of the elevator, Jane looks around the entry hall. "Is the 'modiste' here already?"

I check my phone. "Nope. Mrs. Dubois will be here in ten minutes or so, the others even later."

Jane arches an eyebrow. "The 'modiste' even has a French last name?"

"And an accent to go with it," I say with a grin. "I figured you'd appreciate that."

She shakes her head. "I don't even want to know how much extra you had to pay for the French version."

"As we wait for Mrs. Dubois, would you like a tour of the penthouse?"

Oops. The word 'tour' seems to be a trigger from the gallery debacle—because I can see Jane wince before she puts her poker face back on.

"Sure," she says, although a bit reluctantly. "I know you've been dying to show it all off."

CHAPTER 17

Jane

J ust as we've started to get along, I remember the stupid gallery and the women there, and the green monster inside me reawakens.

It's stupid too, because he's already gotten rid of the paintings and their muses, so what more can I want? A sexist hiring policy for security guards that doesn't allow attractive women? For Adrian to wear a sack over his head so women don't flirt with him? Though given how in-shape he is, they might flirt despite the sack.

"This is the living room," Adrian says.

"You don't say."

He has a TV so big that it could stand in for a movie theater screen. It faces the comfiest-looking couch I've ever seen, as well as an army of uber-expensive, high-end massage chairs/loungers. There are also gaming consoles, a ping pong and a pool table, a bar, and countless other means for what my romance novels call "masculine pursuits."

I spot a bookshelf, so I can't help but check it out. Turns out, it doesn't just hold books. There are also movies, comics, and video games.

I scan them all with my librarian's eye. A lot of the items are about Da Vinci, but just as many are Marvel films, games, and comics featuring Iron Man.

Hmm. There's also an Iron Man poster on the wall —signed by Robert Downey Jr.

"Tony Stark is my favorite character in fiction," Adrian says, following my gaze.

"Is it because he's a vain show-off, like you?"

Adrian's smirk is downright cocky. "Did you forget that he's also arrogant, overconfident, and narcissistic?"

"Why beat a dead horse?" I say, deadpan.

"Tony Stark is good at many things," Adrian says. "And he was able to find something to focus it all on: being Iron Man. I've yet to find my version of that."

His expression, a mixture of longing and self-deprecating humor, tugs at something in my chest, making me want to step closer.

Miss Miller thinks a proper lady should keep her distance, especially in the company of a rake.

"You don't think that's ungrateful?" I ask. "People would sell their souls to the devil to paint as well as you can, or to write music—and so on."

He shrugs. "I'd trade all of it if it meant I'd find something like your passion for books. Or is it libraries?"

"Books," I say definitively. "Have you thought about pursuing something multidisciplinary?"

His eyes light up. "Such as?"

"Maybe become a journalist who covers a bunch of topics? Or a software engineer who writes apps for different fields? Or a teacher of many subjects?"

Adrian's excitement dims. "None of that sounds good to me. When I write, I only write fiction. When I code, it's only as a means to an end of some project. I've never tried teaching, but I don't think that's for me. Plus, it requires advanced degrees, while I'm self-taught in most of the areas I'm interested in."

"You write?" I exclaim, latching on to what matters most to me. "What genre?"

He winks at me. "It's not historical romance, sorry."

"I wouldn't expect you to write that. I don't think you could, even if you wanted to."

He cocks his head. "That sounds like a challenge."

I roll my eyes. "Are you dodging my question on purpose?"

"I'm writing a children's book," he admits. "For Piper."

"You are?" Am I about to swoon, or is this the infamous fit of the vapors? "That's amazing."

"You think so?" His eyes gleam a brighter silver. "I was thinking that if that goes well, I'd make a cartoon out of it, too—and create everything for it myself: the music, the story, the hand-drawn animation, and the CGI."

"There," I say. "If that project goes well, maybe that

could be your thing. You could start with cartoons, then try movies. Sky's the limit, really, and all of it is extremely multidisciplinary."

Adrian rubs his chin thoughtfully. "I don't hate this idea."

His phone rings.

"Ah," he says after glancing at it. "The modiste is downstairs."

I grin. "Seems like the tour will need to be postponed once again."

"But I so want to show off," Adrian says. "Maybe we can do a speed version?" He extends his hand to me, his expression devilish.

I take his hand, my fingers tingling. What have I got to lose?

Miss Miller could name a few things a lady could lose under circumstances such as these: virtue, honor, dignity, and her common sense.

Grinning, Adrian sprints down a corridor, rattling out the names of the rooms. Half of them sound like he's making up rich people clichés, like the pool room, the wine cellar, the gym, the spa, et cetera.

When he says "the library," I halt in my tracks and check if he's telling the truth. After all, there were books in the living room already.

"Oh, my," I gasp as I peek through the double doors.

It's a library bigger than my whole house—one that could contain the library from *Beauty and the Beast* twice over.

"I'm sure you'll spend plenty of time there," Adrian says, gently squeezing my hand. "After all, you're moving in... tomorrow."

CHAPTER 18

Adrian

J ane turns my way, eyelashes flapping like hummingbird wings. "Tomorrow?"

"If that works for you," I say.

Originally, I was going to take things a little slower, but now that I see how perfect she is, I don't want to waste a second.

Perfect for the purposes of the hearing, of course.

She frowns, then shrugs. "It's your show. Are you sure you don't want to make sure I do well at this ball first?"

"No. That's just a silly party." Speaking of... I jokingly smack myself on the forehead. "We totally forgot about Mrs. Dubois."

Jane grins and we sprint to the elevator, where the peacock-bright modiste is already waiting, along with the makeup and hair teams.

"Hello," Mrs. Dubois says disapprovingly, her voice

laced with a heavy French accent. "Did I get the appointment time confused?"

"I'm sorry," Jane says, looking strangely crestfallen—perhaps because this is an unwelcome reminder of yesterday's interview.

Mrs. Dubois eyes her up and down. "Not as sorry as you should be about that outfit."

What the fuck? Does she think she's so good at her job that she can be rude to a client? I'm tempted to fire her on the spot, but we're too close to the event, so I'll have to settle for putting her in her place, which isn't hard since all I have to do is channel my late father.

"I thought I was paying your employers for your time," I say imperiously. "Am I mistaken about that? Doesn't that include waiting time?"

Mrs. Dubois's eyes widen as she nods.

"Then you should be aware that if I wished, I could pay them for a year and just have you wait by this elevator the whole time."

Mrs. Dubois takes a step back. "I didn't mean any disrespect," she says, her French accent fading out and a Boston twang creeping in.

"Perfect," I say. "Do your best with my fiancée, and all will be well."

"Fiancée?" Mrs. Dubois reexamines Jane, and this time, there's undeniable respect in her gaze. "She'll shine, I swear it."

I look at the others. "Same goes for you, right?"

They all agree profusely, and one of them even gives me a military salute.

Dad would be proud, so I feel shitty.

"Set up shop in the living room," I say in a kinder tone. "Jane knows the way." I wink at her. "Meanwhile, I'm going to go take care of some business."

They all head to the living room, and I go to my studio, where I start working on a new project—an animated movie for when Piper is old enough to want to watch such things.

And yes, I admit it, I've been inspired by the conversation with Jane. The plot for the movie is going to be a riff on *Freaky Friday*, *Big*, and other body-swap films, only in this version, it's not a human that the heroine embodies, but a dog. As I type up the script and draw a few sketches of the characters, I enter a state of flow where time flies and the outside world seems to disappear. The heroine is named Piper, of course, and the dog is Leo, which makes drawing them easy: I just picture my daughter a few years older and as a cartoon, and my dog exactly as is.

I'm so lost in the work that when my phone rings, I stare at it in confusion for a second before I answer it.

"I'm all set," Jane says.

Shit. We have to leave soon.

"I'll be right there," I say, and thank the heavens I got a haircut and took a shower back at Jane's place, so all I really need to do is put on a suit.

Hurrying over to my bedroom, I stroll through my closet until I get to the suit section, which is in the farthest corner because I had my assistant organize the whole thing by frequency of wear.

Once I'm dressed, I head toward the library, but as I pass the kitchen, Leo trots up to me, tail wagging.

"Hey, bud," I say. "You hungry?"

He wags his tail harder.

If I ever say 'no' to that question, I'll play tug-of-war with a lion, fall on a sword, or eat a chocolate-covered raisin, whichever happens to be the more convenient way to end things at the time.

I feed him and check my phone to see when the newly hired dog sitter is getting here. Turns out, he's been here for an hour, waiting by the elevator.

I take a dog treat to him to make sure he and Leo click before I go to the library.

Walking in, I realize I might've worked on that animated movie for too long because when I see Jane, I feel like I'm turning into a cartoon wolf—my jaw dropping, eyes boggling, tongue lolling, and Yoda rock-hard.

Spotting me, Jane blushes. "What do you think?"

Oh, fuck. I've been staring, speechless. "You look magnificent," I say and still feel like that's an understatement.

The black dress she has on hugs every curve in just the right way, and the fancy hairdo makes me want to untangle it all and run my fingers through the silky brown strands as I—

"You look rakish," Jane states, but I don't think it's an insult this time. "And you sound like one too."

Ah, so maybe a little bit of an insult, after all.

One of the hair people walks up to me, looking sheepish. "Would you like me to style your hair, sir?"

I glance questioningly at Jane.

"He knows what he's talking about," she says.

I turn to the guy. "Make it quick."

As he does his thing, he asks me if my suit is Ermenegildo Zegna and the shoes Scafora, and I tell him that I honestly don't know—they are whatever my shopping assistant got. All I know is that they were made for me, which involved an annoying waste of time with all the measuring. I've been getting the same suit and shoes ever since, to avoid a repeat of that.

"Okay, done," the guy says after a couple of minutes.

As I glance at the mirror, I don't really see a difference, but I'm not a huge expert on this sort of thing.

"Thoughts?" I ask Jane.

"Even more rakish," she says with a sigh.

"Great. We'd better run." Turning to the crew, I say, "Great job, everyone." To the modiste, I say, "Can we forget about the earlier unpleasantness?"

"What unpleasantness?" she asks, French accent back in play.

With a smile, I grab Jane's hand and drag her to the limo, even though my bedroom seems like a much more tempting destination.

"Is the place far?" Jane asks as we ride down the elevator.

I rip my gaze away from her cleavage. "It's walkable. But since you're in high heels, we'll take the limo."

Speaking of heels, I never noticed how extra sexy women's butts look when they wear these things, or how much—

"A limo?" Jane wipes imaginary dust from my shoulder. "Why forgo taking the helicopter?"

I shrug. "The venue doesn't have a helipad?"

She scoffs. "The scary part is that I'm not sure if you're kidding."

"I was kidding. But there *is* a helipad on my roof, and I do have a helicopter—and I even know how to fly it."

The elevator stops and I gesture for Jane to get out before she can further chastise me for being a rich cliché.

"You said this ball was a fundraiser," Jane says when the limo pulls away. "What's the cause?"

"WSW," I say.

She frowns at me. "Please tell me you don't donate to World Series Wrestling."

"What? No. WSW stands for Whales Save Whales. Uber-wealthy donors, also called whales, donate their money to, well, save the ocean whales."

"Huh," she says. "I like whales. The ocean kind."

The limo stops.

Jane looks at me questioningly. "Are we there already?"

I nod.

She grins. "We really *were* a walking distance away."

With a shrug, I get out and hold the door for her.

As she exits, I enjoy the scent of guava with a hint of begonia—and I have no idea if this is something the makeover team spritzed on her, or if this is Jane herself.

"This way." I offer her my right arm.

"How gentlemanly." She slides her hand through the crook of my elbow.

As we pass my fellow whales inside the venue, I begin to understand something I previously found abhorrent —shallow billionaires who get themselves trophy wives. Jane is so beautiful that I'm proud to parade her on my arm, even if I don't deserve any of said pride. Then again, a trophy wife may be a bad analogy here. People stereotypically think they lack intelligence (even though I know that's not always true—case in point, my mom), but in the case of Jane, she's the sharpest person I've met, and that fact makes me feel even prouder to marry her... or rather, fake-marry her.

"Oh, my," Jane gasps when we step inside the hall. "This is the closest one can get to a ball from one of my novels."

CHAPTER 19

Jane

I stare at my surroundings in awe.

If the palace-like venue had a theme, it would be something like "blue blood." Even the parking valet and the waiters look richer than their usual counterparts. The actual whales downright exude wealth—and make me realize that Adrian is pretty down to Earth in this regard... in comparison to his peers, of course.

"Thoughts?" Adrian whispers.

"This is basically *the ton*," I whisper back. "And I'm a milkmaid."

He rolls his eyes. "You're a diamond of the first order."

"It's water, not order," I say as butterflies somersault in my belly.

"Water?" he asks with a raised eyebrow.

"The brilliance of a diamond is called its water."

Before he can retort, Adrian frowns at something

behind me. When I turn, I see a woman smiling at us like a shark.

With her amber eyes, silky black hair, and small face, she reminds me of what I could've grown up to look like if I had eaten caviar all day from kindergarten on, had had a personal trainer since grade school, and had swum in a pool of gold coins from birth.

But no. In no alternate universe could I manage to look this haughty. If it's true that it takes ten thousand hours to master a task, that must be how long she's had to stare at people down her nose to get this good at it.

"Adrian," she says, her voice dripping with hauteur. "Why would you bring your assistant to The Ball?"

His assistant? Hey, she could have called me his cleaning lady.

Miss Miller finds the term "cleaning lady" quite misleading—maids clean, ladies manage the household. Having said that, even more incongruent would be the term "cleaning gentleman." Oh, and since we're on the subject, the term "crazy cat lady" also raises a lot of questions, like: Why isn't she in Bedlam or locked up in an attic? Are all the cats there to rid her of the mice in said attic, or is she crazy in such a way that she uses them as an aloof source of protein?

"Jane, meet Sydney," Adrian says, sounding more formal than I've ever heard him. "Sydney, meet Jane." He turns to me. "Sydney is Piper's mother."

Oh, crap.

He turns to Sydney. "Jane and I have been secretly

dating for the last six months, and as of yesterday, we're engaged."

Double crap.

Until this moment, Sydney hadn't truly looked at me, but now that she's turned those intense amber eyes on me, I'd rather go back to the good old days when she didn't think me worthy of her notice.

She turns to Adrian, and her fake laugh reminds me of the time Mom tried practicing laughter yoga—which sounded a lot like Jack Nicholson's portrayal of the Joker. "I hope *our daughter* inherits your wonderful sense of humor."

Adrian sighs. "Why would I be joking about that?"

Feeling a little petty, I flash Sydney the ring on my finger.

Her faux joviality is gone without a trace. "You're getting married," she says, enunciating every word.

Adrian crosses his arms over his chest. "Marriage is a common step after getting engaged."

Her eyes narrow. "So now you *are* able to get married?"

Does she want him to tell her outright that he's fine with getting married, just not to her?

Frowning, Adrian turns my way. "Sydney and I are going to talk in private for a moment."

I nod because what else can I do? Even if what Adrian and I have were real, Sydney would still be in his life forever, or at least until their daughter moves out. He needs to stay on talking terms with this woman, and for the next three years, so should I.

Just as they walk away, an unfamiliar middle-aged man approaches me, a champagne flute in his hand.

"Hello." He raises the flute. "I'm Tristan Astor." With that, he extends his hand to me.

I shake the proffered hand. "I'm Jane Miller. I'm sorry... The way you said your name made it sound like I should know it, but I don't."

"Oh." His cheeks flush. "I'm Sydney's father."

Ah. Now that he says it, I can see some resemblance —his hair is the same shade of black, and his eyes are amber. So Sydney's last name is Astor. That could be handy in case I feel like cyberstalking her.

"I saw you talking with her a moment ago," he continues. "So I assumed you were part of the same circle."

He thinks I'm part of the ton? I'll take that as a compliment.

"I'm not part of their circle," I say. "However, since you're Piper's grandfather, our paths might cross again, so we might as well get to know each other."

He looks confused. "How are you connected to Piper?"

Before I can answer, a voice even haughtier than Sydney's says, "Tristan, dear, is that a contender to be wife number four? Or is it five?"

I turn to check out the speaker, a middle-aged lady who looks like she has a team of plastic surgeons on speed dial. She could also easily play an evil dowager baroness in a show about Victorian England.

"Juliet," Tristan says through his teeth. "Tired of your boy toy already?"

Juliet glances at a guy about Adrian's age, then turns back to Tristan. "I'm not actually here to quarrel." She points at Adrian and Sydney in the distance. "Do you think they're reconciling?"

Tristan shrugs and gestures at me. "Maybe Jane has a clue?"

Juliet peers at me and forces one of her perfectly styled eyebrows into a simulacrum of a question mark. "You know my daughter?"

Ah. So this is Sydney's mom, and it seems like she and Tristan aren't together. Probably because her name isn't Isolde, and his name isn't Romeo.

"I just met Sydney a second ago," I say, and don't add that it wasn't a pleasure in the slightest. "I came with Adrian."

"Oh," both of Sydney's parental units say in unison before examining me as if I were a bacterium and they had just invented the microscope.

"*You* came with Adrian?" Juliet continues peering at me. "As a date?"

"I'm his fiancé," I say, figuring it's best to treat this like ripping off a Band-Aid.

They both gape at me in shock, especially Juliet.

"I thought it'd be just a matter of time before he'd wake up and marry Sydney," Juliet says, more to Tristan than to me.

"And I thought he didn't want to marry her because

he was afraid of the commitment," Tristan says. "But he's marrying someone else?"

Do I need to be a part of this conversation?

Juliet's eyes zero in on me. "Do you have a child with him also?"

"Not that I know of." Grr. What does that even mean?

"Then why?" they ask in unison.

"You'll have to ask Adrian," I say, and thank my lucky stars because in that moment, I spot him coming our way.

Poor guy.

He's just gotten out of the Sydney frying pan, just to get tossed into the fire of Tristan and Juliet.

CHAPTER 20
Adrian

"What the actual fuck?" Sydney demands as soon as we're just barely out of Jane's earshot.

"Excuse me? Is that supposed to be something I'm able to answer?"

"Are you taunting me?" she demands.

"Again, I'm not sure what you're talking about," I say.

She looks ready to shoot lightning with her eyes. "I invite you to a party, and you bring some rando."

I sigh. "Jane is not a rando. As I told you, we've been dating for six months."

"Bullshit. I'd know it if that were the case."

"With what, your 'psychic' powers?"

She narrows her eyes into tiny slits. "You *know* I'm an intuitive."

"Intuitive is not a noun." If she had any intuition at

all, it would tell her how awful our married life would be. And that crystals don't work.

She takes a deep breath. "Look, when you met her isn't important. What's important is that *we* have a baby together."

I do my best to calm myself as well. For Piper's sake, the two of us need to learn to get along... somehow. "She doesn't want us to marry. Trust me."

Sydney takes a step toward me, eyes gleaming. "Having a mommy *and* a daddy is the thing she wants most. You wouldn't know anything different because your parents stayed together. Mine split when I turned five. It was terrible."

This is a conversation we've had a million times. Sydney truly suffered when Tristan and Juliet got divorced, but she doesn't care when I tell her that my situation was the exact opposite. My mom *should* have left my dad, and everyone would've been happier, but she didn't.

"Piper *will* have both a mommy and a daddy," I say conciliatorily. "I plan to be in her life. That's the whole point of—"

"No," Sydney hisses. "She'll be better off if she doesn't even know your name."

With that, she stomps off.

Fuck. A part of me had hoped that when Sydney learned that I've moved on, she'd do the same and abandon her delusions of marrying me. And, of course, stop fighting me on custody. I guess that would've been too easy.

Anyway, I've left Jane alone for far too long. I turn back to her—and can't believe my eyes. Sydney's parents have cornered her like a pack of rabid hyenas.

As I rush over, Jane's face lightens with relief, so I know I'm just in time.

"You didn't reconcile, did you?" Tristan says, skipping the usual pleasantries.

Out of the two, I like Tristan more, so I choose my words carefully. "I'm afraid your daughter and I have irreconcilable differences."

There. That's much better than saying that his daughter is vapid, shallow, and vain—and that he and his ex-wife messed her up so badly she'd rather deprive Piper of her father than have an amicable shared custody arrangement.

"What a shame," Tristan says. "If you never get the chance to speak with Piper again, you'll regret it."

My hands ball into fists, and I take a step forward without meaning to. "Was that a threat?"

Tristan takes a step back. "A statement of fact. There's no guarantee you'll get custody."

I relax my hands. The last thing I want is to smack Piper's grandfather. Something like that would seal the custody case for sure. "I will get custody," I say evenly. "The judge will see that I want what's best for Piper."

"No, you won't," Juliet says nastily. "The judges always favor the mother."

She has a point. Even though they're supposed to consider both parents equally, judges are human and have human biases, so they often do favor the mother, despite the letter of the law.

I take a calming breath just as Jane puts a reassuring hand on my shoulder. Her touch helps tremendously. My tone is almost pleasant as I address both of Sydney's parents. "Can you help Sydney realize that what's best for Piper is for her to know her father?"

Juliet scoffs. "Nothing will help you after this insult." She glances at Jane.

That, right there, is but a taste of why Tristan must've run from her.

"I don't understand your meaning," I say frostily. "Nor do I care to."

Juliet puts her hands on her hips. "The insult is you announcing that you're going to marry a woman who looks like a cheap imitation of the one who bore you a child."

"Jane couldn't be more different from Sydney if someone had genetically engineered her to be so," I state. Turning to Jane, I add, "I mean that as a compliment."

Jane blushes while Juliet's eyes turn laser-like. Yep, that's where Sydney inherited that from.

I meet her stare for stare. "Now, you'll have to excuse us." I turn to Jane and extend my hand. "May I have this dance?"

Clearly ecstatic to be out of this unpleasant situation, Jane beams at me. "I'd love that."

As I lead her away, she whispers, "A dance without music?"

Winking at her, I swing by the DJ's table, slip him a few hundreds, airdrop him a file, and reunite with Jane.

"Music issue remedied," I say. "The DJ was going to start in a half hour or so anyway, so I've merely hastened matters."

The music starts playing.

Jane's eyes widen. "Is this a remix of the theme from *Bridgerton*?"

I smile. "Not exactly. It's something that I wrote—heavily inspired by it."

She bites her lip. "You wrote this?"

"I had a feeling you might enjoy dancing to it." And right now, I have a feeling her plump, juicy lips would be very fun to nibble on.

"Right." She looks around at a few people who are already with us on the dance floor. "Shall we?"

Fuck. Between the lip biting and us getting this close, Yoda's lightsaber is extending. Then again, we must be seen as a couple, and dancing speaks volumes.

I take her hands in mine and begin waltzing, but I keep a distance to make sure she doesn't feel the effect that she's having on me.

The next song is faster, so we're dancing apart, and I get to watch her sway her hips as her perfect round breasts bob up and down to the music—in other words, not an improvement over being too close as far as inappropriate thoughts and urges go.

By song five, it's official.

If I keep dancing with Jane, my balls will resemble a blue robin's eggs.

CHAPTER 21

Jane

I don't believe that the Spanish fly is an aphrodisiac that turns women into nymphomaniacs, but if it were, it would feel a lot like the way dancing with Adrian makes me feel. I'm not sure if it's the closeness, his bespoke suit, or the intensity in his silver eyes, but my glasses keep fogging up, as well as my panties. Relatedly, he moves with such rhythm and precision that he can add "dancer" to his already-long list of things he's amazing at.

Miss Miller believes that dancing in general—and the waltz in particular—isn't something that an unmarried lady should indulge in. Nor should a lady dance with the same gentleman so many times in a row. Nor—

The music stops. I suppress my crushing disappointment. Turns out, I'm one of those girls who could dance the whole night away—who knew?

"People are about to pledge their donations," Adrian explains. "Lots of showing-off is about to ensue."

I nod knowingly. "That means you *have* to be there."

He grins. "Actually, I already donated online."

"I guess when you're rich *enough* and everyone knows it, you don't need to publicly flaunt your wealth. You've got nothing to prove."

His grin widens. "Don't let the other members of the one percent hear you—you might start a new trend."

Why is my chest feeling so light? "This stays between us," I say conspiratorially. "What should we do now?"

Example: go to some club to dance.

"Want to talk in the lounge area?" He extends his arm to me.

Since I'm not brave enough to push for more dancing, I accept his arm, and we promenade to the area in question where a waiter tempts us with a tray of champagne.

Adrian grabs a drink, so I follow his lead.

"What do you think of the event so far?" Adrian asks.

I sip the champagne—and it's divine, of course. "In my favorite books, they would call it 'the squeeze of the season.'"

He chuckles. "That sounds like we're talking about orange juice."

I take another sip of champagne and shock myself by asking, "So what's the deal with you and Sydney?"

Why not marry her for real? She's attractive and rich, and only slightly bitchy.

Adrian blows out a breath. "She and I went to prep school together—insert joke about entitled rich kids here."

I snort. "If anyone makes fun of prep schools, it's because they're jealous they couldn't get their kids into them, or themselves. That or they watched too much *Gossip Girl*."

"Right," he says. "Sydney was one of the mean girls back in school, which I found abhorrent back then—and my opinion on it only worsened over the years. We were both popular kids, so she decided that she wanted me as a feather in her cap, but I wasn't interested so she dropped the pursuit." He sighs. "Cut to about a year ago when I was in a phase of my life when I partied too much. I was at a club on molly—the drug, not a woman—and bumped into Sydney. It started off as us asking each other about what happened to so-and-so from our school days, and then the rest played out like a 'Just Say No' ad: I fucked a woman I despise, got her pregnant, and here we are."

My head spins, and not just from the magnificent champagne. He told me before that she'd lied about having an IUD—and that she might've poked a hole in the condom they used, which means she never gave up on her prep school ambition.

I put a hand on his leg—a reassuring gesture that has nothing to do with wanting to feel the powerful muscle under my fingertips. "I get why you don't want to marry her."

"If I thought marrying her would actually benefit Piper, I'd make that sacrifice," he says. "But it would only harm our daughter. Even marriages based on love end in divorce half the time, so what chance would I have with a woman who is like the oil to my water?"

I squeeze his leg—again, not because I'm a perv. "I wasn't judging you for not wanting to."

"The crazy thing is, even if a time machine existed, I wouldn't change that night—not after meeting Piper."

"I get it," I say as my heart tightens in my chest.

I'm glad Piper has a father who loves her this much, but I'm also jealous and curious about what it must be like.

Adrian covers my hand with his. "The two of us have only known each other for two days, yet I'm confident that if our marriage were to be real, we'd have a much better chance than me and the mother of my child. How sad is that?"

I stare at him, my heart now fluttering somewhere around my uvula. Did he just say that we'd be good together for real? No, can't be. He's just contrasting me with the woman that he despises, so naturally, I come out the winner.

Pulling my hand away from his, I down my champagne and feel bubbles assaulting my nose.

"Sorry," he says and waves at the nearby waiter to get me another flute. "I don't mean to be a downer tonight."

"You're not a downer," I say, accepting the drink. "Besides, I was the one who asked."

"You did," he says. "Which means now it's your turn."

"For what?"

His silver eyes seem to penetrate into my soul and all

the way down to my coccyx as he says, "Tell me about you. What do you like?"

I cock my head. "You mean besides books?"

Sipping his drink, he nods.

"I like classical music." I move my glasses higher up my nose. "And you already know about my movie watching with my mom, as well as—"

"No," he says with a headshake. "Tell me something more intimate."

A blush spreads over my cheeks. "If you mean former relationships, there isn't much to tell. Back in high school, I went on a couple of dates, but I was too busy in college with studying. My plan was to get on something like Tinder once I became a librarian." At which point I'd have my GD—but there's no way I'm bringing that up again, especially not when the champagne is making me feel like I want Adrian to handle that particular task.

"I'm sorry you're not going to get the chance to date for the next couple of years," he says, but he doesn't look like he means it.

If anything, there's an almost satisfied gleam in his silver eyes.

I frown, then decide I'm imagining it. "It's fine. Getting on Tinder doesn't mean I'd actually meet anyone."

He rolls his eyes. "You'd have to swat men away with a stick. Trust me."

Is it the champagne bubbles again, or are there drunk butterflies in my stomach?

"Tell me an embarrassing secret," he says.

I smile weakly. "You mean besides being a virgin?"

"Yeah, that one isn't embarrassing in the slightest."

"Fine," I say—and can't believe I'm about to admit this. "I often think about myself in third person, where I roleplay a Victorian lady named Miss Miller." He's already grinning, but I go on. "I also always dress up as Miss Miller for Halloween and have more corsets than a dominatrix."

His grin turns devilish. "Just Halloween? Be honest."

My face is so hot it must be a shade of pink only bees can see. "Sometimes I dress up that way just as a pick-me-up."

His eyes grow hooded. "Once you move in tomorrow, you're welcome to promenade around my apartment in cosplay any time you want. In fact, I'll pay you an extra million dollars if you do so."

"Oh, God. I completely forgot about the move."

He waves his hand dismissively. "I hired the best movers money can buy. They'll take care of everything. You don't need to worry."

Yeah, no. The logistics of moving aren't what I'm worried about. It's living with the proverbial sex on a stick.

Miss Miller will henceforth forgo eating anything on sticks ever again, including but not limited to: ice cream, kebabs, and—just in case—a sandwich if it's held together by a toothpick.

"I think you're trying to trick me," I say as a way to change the topic to something less blush-worthy. "I told you my embarrassing secret. You have to tell me yours."

"Right," he says. "But before I do, I have to remind you about the NDA."

I bite my lip. "You make it sound juicy."

He takes in a big breath, then blurts out, "I can't swim."

I wait for some sort of punchline, but it never comes. "You don't know how to swim?"

"I know how. I just can't."

"That makes no sense." I gulp my drink, but that only makes the whole issue murkier.

Miss Miller does not think getting foxed on champagne will improve a lady's skills at conversation.

Adrian shrugs. "Cats can instinctively swim, but few like to get wet."

"But you have a pool room in your place," I say. "Or was that a joke?"

"Oh, I have a pool," he says. "But ever since the thing with my parents, I won't get into pools, or any other body of water bigger than a bathtub. Relatedly, I don't go onto pool floats, boats, cruise ships, ferries, giant ducks—or anything else that goes over the surface of water."

I was just about to tease him about this mercilessly, but if it has to do with his parents' deaths, I won't even smile.

"The pool is now a ball pit," he continues. "But the name of the room kind of stuck."

Now I grin. "You have a pool-sized ball pit?"

"It's actually very fun, and I'm sure Piper will appreciate it when she's older."

I feel that pull toward him again. I think it's the way his eyes lit up when he mentioned his daughter's name. He must feel it too because his eyes flare and darken, and he leans toward me.

Heavens. Our lips are close. So close I feel the heat coming from his.

And then the damned music turns on again.

Adrian snaps out of whatever spell came over us and straightens. "Seems like the pledging is done. Would you like to dance?"

I would, but I shouldn't. This already feels too much like a date. If we dance any longer, my heart is going to get even more confused.

I shift away from him on the couch. "I'd better go home so I can get good sleep tonight. Before the move and all."

"Ah. Of course. I'll take you now."

Should I be flattered by how disappointed he looks and sounds?

"Have the limo take me," I say, feeling like a coward. "There's no reason for you to personally shlep to Staten Island and back."

His face is hard to read. "If that's what you want."

"It is," I lie.

Standing up, he offers me his elbow again, and we walk to the car. As we approach it, my heartbeat skyrockets. The night has felt so much like a date that if he were to try to kiss me at the end, it wouldn't surprise me in the slightest. It would give me palpitations, but wouldn't surprise me.

He opens the door. "Have a safe trip."

He leans in.

I almost have a heart attack.

He pecks me on the forehead—because of course he does.

I slink into the car, my cheeks so hot you could fry an omelet on them.

On the trip back, I replay everything that's happened since I met Adrian, and it feels like a dream.

And tomorrow, I'll move in with him. This fact is difficult to even wrap my mind around—but I try, for the whole ride home.

When I walk into the house, Mom and Mary demand every detail, so I tell them, and by the time I'm done, I start to yawn.

"Go to sleep," Mom says when Mary matches my yawn with one of her own.

Good idea. I go through all my nightly rituals and get into bed—which is when sleep decides to become elusive.

Fine. It seems I'm too wired and have too much Adrian swirling through my busy mind.

So be it. I begin a new novel, and it keeps me busy until I get to the very shmexy scene where the rakish duke rips off the heroine's bodice.

I close the book.

I have an idea about how to make myself sleepy and release some of the tension Adrian has caused.

Miss Miller can foresee what is coming and must prophylactically reach for the smelling salts.

Yep. Just because I'm a virgin doesn't mean I don't

masturbate—which is exactly what I need if I want to get any shut-eye tonight.

I reach under the blanket and begin brushing my fingers over my clit—and as I do, I picture Adrian as the duke from the book and myself as the bodice-less lady.

Boom. The orgasm bursts through me like a cork out of a well-shaken champagne bottle.

Finally satisfied, I fall asleep, and Adrian appears to me in a dream, naked and hard. Naturally, he deflowers me, and there's only one word that can describe the act.

Grand.

CHAPTER 22

Adrian

I wake up with a single thought on my mind: Jane is
moving in, in mere hours.

Working with my cleaning lady, I make sure
the house is spotless, particularly the bigger of the guest
rooms, henceforth known as Jane's room.

Your movers are here, Jane informs me via text. *Did
you pay them extra to make sure I wouldn't lift a finger?
Because I haven't.*

I grin.

*No, but I'm going to pay them extra now. I like the
idea that the move is going to be easy for you.*

We text like that for the duration of her move, and
then the movers descend on my apartment like a plague
of very polite and diligent locusts.

They not only bring the stuff in but ask Jane where
she wants everything laid out, and then they do as she
says in such a tidy way that even Marie Kondo would
approve.

"Well," I say to Jane when the invasion is over. "I want to officially welcome you to my humble abode."

She looks around her new room—which is about the size of her townhouse on Staten Island. "Humble. Sure."

Leo trots in and starts sniffing Jane's things.

"See?" I say in his voice. "When I tripped the nice-smelling lady, I knew what I was doing."

Jane chuckles and ruffles the fur on Leo's head.

"Let me show you around," I say. "I don't think you entered most of the rooms during the earlier tour."

She agrees, and I take her to all the rooms, the last one being the pool/ball pit area.

"It's exactly as I imagined," she says after examining the million and one multi-colored balls. "And it still smells a little bit like chlorine."

I narrow my eyes at Leo. "Someone drools excessively over the balls when he plays in the pit, so the cleaning people are forced to use chlorine to disinfect the place from time to time."

I'm not sure what Leo imagines I said to him just then, but for whatever reason, he rushes at me, tail wagging madly.

I don't care what you say—you're the best. And you smell nice. And—

Fuck. I'm on the edge of the pit, waving my arms around like a scarecrow in a hurricane, praying it helps me regain my balance.

Jane leaps toward me and grabs my hand.

Nope. All she accomplishes is dragging herself down with me as I finally fall.

Plop.

The fall doesn't hurt, of course. It's fun, in fact—especially the part where Jane ends up on top of me, her breath frantic and eyes wild.

"I'm so sorry," I say as soon as I catch *my* breath.

"I'm not," she says, then rolls off me and dives into the balls.

Grinning, I dive in too, and Leo jumps in after us.

The next ten minutes are the kind of fun you can only have during childhood. We laugh so hard that my jaw hurts, and Jane's makeup runs from happy tears. For Leo, this is a regular Monday, of course.

"As soon as Piper is old enough, you have to let her do this," Jane says after we climb out and rest on the nearby lounge chairs.

"Definitely," I say, and feel a pang of anxiety at the reminder that I could lose my custody battle and never get the chance to play with Piper here or anywhere else.

Leo climbs out of the ball pit with a yellow ball in his mouth—which is his favorite color.

"I like to play with Piper too," Leo says. "And sniff her. And lick her. She's superior to Adrian in every way."

Jane chuckles, and then her stomach rumbles, to which she responds by turning redder than any of the balls in the pit.

"Sorry," she says. "I guess I'm a bit peckish."

I take her to the kitchen and serve her a crab cake sandwich with what I claim to be leftovers. In reality, I made everything fresh for her earlier today.

When she takes a bite, her eyes roll back into her head

—which causes a stirring in my Yoda region because that is probably what Jane's O-face looks like.

Yoda doesn't feel any better when she swallows.

Or when she takes another bite.

And another.

Even when she drinks a sip of water, she makes it somehow look erotic.

"So," she says when the sandwich is gone. "What are you up to today?"

Ah. Right. Getting back to the mundane is a good way to calm things down in the libido department.

I hope.

"Piper is visiting tomorrow," I say. "So I was thinking of setting up some more decorations in the nursery."

Jane narrows her eyes theatrically. "You haven't shown me the nursery."

"It's a big apartment," I say, doing my best not to sound too guilty. The truth is, out of all my recent projects, the nursery is what I feel most insecure about. I'm a guy, and Piper's my first baby, so what do I know about readying a room for an infant in general, let alone a little girl?

Jane leaps to her feet. "Show it to me. Now."

CHAPTER 23

Jane

As we enter the nursery, the awe makes me forget to breathe for a second.

The room is magnificent in a cute, adorable, and over-the-top way.

Instead of a regular ceiling, there's a dome reminiscent of a planetarium, with stars and a moon that look more realistic than anything you can spot in the NYC sky. There are also planets flying around, and they look so three-dimensional I ask Adrian if they're holograms.

"They're paper globe replicas hung on very thin wires," he explains. "I set up a mechanical pulley system so that they move just as they do in the real world."

"Of course you did," I say as I gape around some more. The south wall of the room is covered in real-looking butterflies of seemingly every species and color imaginable. Oh, and they are flapping their wings, of course. Similarly, the north wall is teeming with birds, the west wall has animals (with sound effects), and the east wall is blooming with more flowers than a botanical garden.

"How?" I ask, pointing at the walls.

"High-end screens," he says. "I had some of the inventions in this room patented, so that other parents will be able to do this in a few years."

"Wow." I peer at a stylishly futuristic *something* in the corner. "Is that the crib?"

He nods. "It's smart, so it tracks all her vitals and adjusts things like the temperature in the room and the firmness of the mattress for her ultimate comfort. Also, it will automatically rock her to sleep as soon as she starts to wake up at night."

I've never seen such a glaring physical manifestation of parental love.

"Piper is one lucky baby," I say reverently.

He turns to me, eyes gleaming. "You really think so? I feel terrible that she's going to be bouncing between Sydney and me."

"She's a kid," I say. "It might actually be a fun adventure to spend time here and there. I loved going to my grandparents when I was a kid. This will be similar."

"I hope you're right," he says.

"She'll love this," I say confidently. "Just look around."

He does, and his eyes light up. "I just had an idea. I'm going to add shooting stars to the sky, so she can wish upon them."

I grin. "How about you go implement that? Meanwhile, I'll settle into my room."

"Great idea," he says and rushes off.

I scan the nursery again, sigh in amazement, and stroll over to my room.

On the way, I spot a door to a room he never showed me.

I peek in.

Ah. It's his bedroom.

How wrong would it be if I went inside, took a look in the drawers, and—though I'm not sure why—smelled his pillow?

Miss Miller considers that—hopefully rhetorical—question objectionable on many grounds, with moral being just the pinnacle of them.

My phone rings.

It's Mary.

"Hi, sis," I say.

Forgoing any pleasantries, Mary assaults my ears with an avalanche of questions, of which I only catch, "How much do you like the place? Is it amazing? Have you unpacked all your stuff?"

"Slow down," I say, and begin answering the best I can. As soon as I cover some of the questions, Mary produces another bunch.

Midway through all this, I get another call.

It's Mom.

"Hey," I say to Mary. "I'll call you back in a few."

When I pick up Mom's call, she hits me with almost the same questions, but with more innuendo, or at least I assume that's why she asks, "How *big* is it?"

"Put me on speaker so I don't have to repeat myself for Mary," I grumble.

"I'm not near her at the moment," Mom says.

I roll my eyes. "Then can this wait until you are?"

"No chance," Mom says. "Now, dish."

Fine. I allow the interrogation. As soon as I hang up, my phone rings again.

Must be Mary. I forgot to call her back. Annoyed beyond measure, I accept the call, and in my snarkiest tone, I say, "If you keep this up, you'll grow up to be an even bigger gossip than your mother."

Someone who sounds nothing like Mary clears her throat on the other line. "My mother is deceased, and sadly, I've been done with growing for many years now."

Oh, shit.

Why is that voice familiar?

"Now," the speaker continues, "do I have the wrong number, or did you think I was someone else?"

I finally recognize who is speaking, and my feet freeze to the floor. "Mrs. Corsica?" As in, the woman from the horror show that was my library interview?

"Ah, so it *is* Jane Miller," Mrs. Corsica says with a chill in her tone that matches my foot situation perfectly.

"I'm so sorry," I say. "I thought you were my younger sister and accepted the call without looking."

"I see," she says, her tone not a degree warmer. "That would explain what you said—assuming your mother *is* a gossip."

"Again, I'm sorry," I say while a question swirls through my brain.

Why is Mrs. Corsica calling me in the first place?

There can be only one explanation. Despite how poorly I performed at the interview, she wanted to offer me my dream job, after all. Wanted—past tense—because after what I've just said, the offer must be caput.

"My late mother was also a gossip," Mrs. Corsica shocks me by saying. "Long before Facebook, if I wanted an update on anyone, all I had to do was mention them around her. She always had their latest relationship status and other juicy news."

I pull the phone away from my ear to make sure this isn't some prank. Nope. The library is listed as the caller, which means that the ice queen herself has just shared a personal detail with me.

"You must miss her," I say cautiously.

"Very much," Mrs. Corsica says, her tone just a degree above frostbite. "Anyway..." She clears her throat once more. "Let us get back to my reason for calling."

Dare I hope? After all that?

"We have considered your application carefully," Mrs. Corsica says stiffly. "And we've decided to extend you a job offer."

I know I'm probably risking the job yet again, but I squeal like a teen upon seeing her boy band idol.

Mrs. Corsica sighs grumpily. "Your abundance of enthusiasm for the role was actually one of the deciding factors. But please bear in mind that when facing the public, you're going to be expected to act with decorum and poise."

Mrs. Corsica would make the ideal chaperone for Miss

Miller, or any young lady of good breeding and genteel disposition.

I straighten my spine and bite my tongue to prevent any more squealing. "Of course. Decorum will be my motto. Poise too."

"Good," she says. "When can you start?"

"Tomorrow," I blurt excitedly. In a much calmer tone, I add, "Or whenever it is convenient for you."

"Tomorrow is fine," she says. "Now let's talk numbers."

"Sure."

She names a salary, and I do something that all self-help books on job searching do *not* recommend—accept the offer on the spot. And hey, why not? Thanks to my upcoming fake marriage, I don't have to worry about paying my bills.

"I'm glad we've come to a mutually acceptable arrangement," Mrs. Corsica says. "Come by tomorrow for your first day, and you can sign all the paperwork at the same time."

"I'll be there." Even though Mrs. Corsica can't see me, I salute her, like a soldier would a general.

"Oh, and I know it's self-evident at this point, but bear in mind that punctuality is extremely important for the job," Mrs. Corsica says. "As is looking presentable."

"I'll get there early," I say solemnly. "And bring a spare outfit in case another dog pushes me into the mud."

"It's possible that you will *not* make me regret this decision," Mrs. Corsica says. "See you tomorrow."

Listening to the end-of-call tone, I wonder how big a compliment it must be for Mrs. Corsica to say she might *not* regret hiring me.

When it comes from a dragon such as that, Miss Miller considers it high praise indeed.

Giddy with excitement, I let my feet carry me into the kitchen, where I bump into Leo, who is drinking water from his bowl.

"I got the job," I tell the dog. "Can you believe it?"

Leo cocks his head and wags his tail.

"Where's Adrian? Or do you think of him as Dad?"

Leo's ears perk up and he runs out of the kitchen. I follow. When we reach the elevator, I watch in fascination as Leo smacks the elevator button with his furry paw.

Huh. This sheep-like creature is smarter than I would've guessed.

When the elevator arrives, Leo leaps into it and presses the button for Adrian's studios.

Seriously smart.

As soon as we reach our destination, Leo wags his tail and runs out into the hallway. I hurry after him. Soon, we reach the room where Adrian is working on something.

"Sorry to interrupt," I say when Adrian takes his headphones off.

"I was almost done," he says. "What happened? You're glowing."

"I got the job," I blurt. Then, overwhelmed with

positive emotions, I run up to my husband-to-be and peck him on the cheek.

Adrian holds his cheek as though I've burned or slapped it. "What job?"

Crap. I shouldn't have invaded his personal space like that.

"The library called," I say, my face undoubtedly red. "And made me an offer."

He frowns. "The job Leo allegedly ruined for you?"

I ruffle the fur on the dog's head. "I guess he didn't ruin it, after all. Sorry about that."

Adrian's frown morphs into a smile. "That's wonderful."

"I know, right?" I resist the urge to peck him again, or more.

"We have to celebrate," Adrian states.

I bob my head. "Definitely. But not too hard— tomorrow is my first day."

He flashes his white teeth in a grin. "We'll do whatever you want."

Oh, the images. In a flash, I see us celebrating in bed, with candles all around and him making my every fantasy come true.

He cocks his head, vaguely Leo-like. "You have something specific in mind, don't you?"

"Yes." My face now feels like one of the imaginary candles has set it on fire.

He looks particularly roguish as he demands, "What would you like to do?"

"*Bridgerton*," I say.

Obviously, there's no way I'd tell him what I just realized I "really want."

I want him to help me rid myself of virginity.

More specifically, I want him to be the one to perform the GD.

CHAPTER 24

Adrian

"**B**ridgerton?" I stare at Jane in confusion.

"Yes."

"But... what about it?" I recall her admission about owning—and wearing—corsets, to Yoda's dismay.

"I want to watch it," she clarifies.

"You want to watch Netflix," I say slowly. "To celebrate?"

With her being a virgin, I doubt she'd even know about Netflix and chill, let alone choose that as her celebration of choice.

She puts her hands on her hips. "Why not?"

"Because you've seen it already?" And because there's an infinite number of activities that are more celebratory, like eating cake, lobster, or Jane's sweet pussy.

"I've only seen season two four times," Jane says. "To catch up to season one, I've got five more watches to go."

I scratch my head. "If that's what you want. Should we open a bottle of wine?"

I think I've got just the vintage for such a special occasion.

"Wine would be nice," she says. "And maybe a cheese plate."

"I'll make you a plate," I say. "The only thing is, I don't currently have any cheese made from cow's milk."

"You don't? What animal does your cheese come from?"

"Donkey, moose, and water buffalo. All tasty."

"Oh, sure. They all sound *very* appetizing." She glances at Leo. "What about cheese made from sheep?"

"You mean Feta cheese?"

She blinks at me. "Is that what that's made from?"

I nod. "The best ones have seventy percent ewes' milk and the rest goat." After a pause, I add, "Ewe is a female sheep."

"Eww indeed." She grimaces. "I wonder who came up with the idea of milking random animals and then drinking it?"

I smile. "Don't forget waiting for that milk to curdle in the case of cheese. That sounds even crazier."

She grins. "I bet it was someone like you."

"I'll take that as a compliment," I say, though I'm not sure if I should. "Let's go."

We swing by the wine cellar and grab the bottle I had in mind.

"Romanée-Conti," Jane reads from the bottle. "Is it expensive?"

"Not to me," I say with a handwave and head for the fridge.

Turns out, we're in luck. Not only do I locate the cheeses I mentioned, but I do have a small piece of cow-based cheese from Pearl Hyman, a talented local cheesemaker.

We settle on the couch, wine glasses in hand, and I turn on the TV.

Jane takes a sip of her wine and gasps. "This is so good! How can wine be this good?"

"Try the cheese." Or don't. If that sexy gasping continues, Yoda might just lose his shit.

Jane gingerly picks up a piece of cheese, then moans in pleasure—as I feared she might.

"Wow," she says. "I don't care if they had to milk subway rats to make this. It's delicious."

She samples a different cheese and moans from that too.

Disturbing to Yoda, that moaning is.

To drown it out, I start the show.

It doesn't help. During the first half of the first episode, Jane's enjoyment of the wine and cheese keeps me in a constant state of arousal. Once the food is gone, I don't get a break either. She scoots closer to me, close enough for me to smell her, and then she tucks her little feet under her shapely butt.

Oh, and did I mention how she moistens her lips whenever there's kissing on the screen? Or how warm her dainty shoulder feels when it touches mine?

When I can't take another minute of this, I pause the show. "It's getting late."

Still cuddled into me, Jane turns her head, and even her eyes look sexy—pupils dilated, lids heavy. "I *do* have to wake up early for my first day on the new job."

"There you go," I say, and before I do anything that I'd later regret, I leap to my feet—a mistake, Yoda-wise.

If Jane notices my tenting pants, she doesn't show it. Instead, she wishes me a good night and walks away, her hips swaying maddeningly.

I count to four Mississippi, then run to my bedroom, where I vigorously scratch Yoda behind the ears.

CHAPTER 25

Jane

In historical romances, the heroines sometimes feel a throbbing in their wombs, which I always thought was a fanciful way to say "horny." Tonight, on that couch, that is exactly what happened to me. That, and my breasts felt tender, and there was a gnawing emptiness in my core.

By the end of the first episode, I almost begged Adrian to GD me, but I obviously chickened out.

Still, there's always tomorrow. Or the day after.

All I know is, Adrian seems like a man who knows what he's doing in that department, and I've always dreamed of having an orgasm my first time, which is probably difficult because of the pain and discomfort usually associated with the act. I figure since I'll already remember Adrian for the rest of my life as the man who gave me financial security, why not remember this extra factoid about him—that he was my deflowerer? I bet it will be a memory I'll cherish.

The more I think about it, the less crazy the idea seems.

Equal parts excited and unsettled, I head to bed. Naturally, sleep doesn't come. Between the new bed, the new job, and Adrian, I'm all but buzzing with adrenaline.

Which is why I have to self-administer three orgasms to have the slightest chance of shut-eye.

I skip like a kid on my commute to work, which consists of a five-minute walk, courtesy of my new domicile. If I were coming from Staten Island, it would be a two-hour ordeal involving a bus, a ferry, and a couple of trains.

To my shock, Mrs. Corsica smiles when she greets me. Granted, it's only for a millisecond and with just the corners of her eyes, but still, a miracle.

She has me start with some boring red tape, but once I'm done, my first workday proceeds so wonderfully I almost want to pinch myself. Especially when she has me sort the historical romance collection that got me interested in this particular library in the first place.

As my workday draws to a close, I almost don't want to leave.

When should I leave?

I wait until everyone else is gone before heading over to Mrs. Corsica's office—where the door is currently ajar.

Mrs. Corsica is laser focused on her screen.

This is probably a bad time.

I turn to leave, but she clears her throat.

"Hi," I say guiltily, turning around. "I was wondering if there was anything else I need to do?"

"No. You can go home. Good job."

I don't just go home—I float there, buoyed by that "good job."

As I enter Adrian's penthouse—correction, *our* penthouse, temporarily—I recall that today is the first time I'm going to meet Piper. That means I probably shouldn't ask him about my GD just yet.

His dad duties seem more important.

"Hey," Adrian says, coming around the corner. "How was it?"

"Amazing," I say. "Where's Piper?"

He looks at his phone. "Sydney is late, as usual."

I can tell that this bothers him a lot more than he's letting on.

Poor guy.

To distract him, I suggest we eat dinner together, and once we sit down at the kitchen table, I talk his ear off about my new job.

"What about you?" I ask, shoveling the last of the scallops into my mouth. "What were you up to?"

"I started to babyproof some of the rooms," he says and looks at his phone again.

I grin. "Is Piper crawling already?"

"Not yet, but I wanted to get a head start."

Adrian's phone pings. He checks it and looks relieved. "Sydney just texted," he says. "They're here."

He rushes to the elevator, and I don't know if I should follow, but Leo herds me like he would a fellow sheep, so I don't have a choice.

When we reach our destination, Sydney is smiling coquettishly at Adrian. As she spots me, her eyes narrow and lips turn down in a scowl.

"What is she doing here?" she demands.

Adrian sighs. "We went over this already. Jane is my fiancée. Obviously, we live together."

Sydney grabs on to the handlebar of the stroller so hard her knuckles turn white. "If she's going to be around my daughter, I need to run a background check."

"*Our* daughter," Adrian says as he pulls up his phone and makes a few swipes. Looking back at Sydney, he says, "I ran a background check on Jane after we got serious. The results are in your inbox. Anything else?"

She reads whatever he sent her and mumbles something about doing her own investigation as soon as she gets the chance, but her hands relax their death grip on that handlebar.

"Here." She takes off a backpack and hands it to Adrian in such a way that their fingers brush.

Do background checks say anything about murderous urges one sometimes gets when a baby mama touches one's fake fiancé?

"There's a batch of breastmilk in here," Sydney says. "Warm it to ninety-eight degrees exactly and make sure it doesn't boil."

For the first time, Adrian's chilly façade breaks. "Don't worry Syd," he says soothingly. "Piper was fine with me the last time, and she'll be fine today. I know what I'm doing. I've read all the books and taken all the classes. Just relax."

Sydney's eyes turn icy. "Don't tell me how to feel. You're not a mother. You have no idea what it's like to part with your baby."

Adrian's jaw flexes. "I've got laboratory-grade equipment for the milk that will warm it to 36.6 degrees Celsius—exactly normal body temperature. Do you want to inspect it? Test it out?"

"No," she says. "But promise you'll call me if something happens."

"Nothing will happen," Adrian says. "But if anything does, you'll be the first to know."

"Bye, sweetie," Sydney says into the stroller with such tenderness I forgive her for the earlier nastiness... but not for touching Adrian. I'm not a saint.

A part of me was worried that Sydney saw this baby only as a means to trap Adrian. Now it seems that even if that had been the starting point, Sydney loves their daughter as a mother should.

When Sydney looks up from the stroller, her gaze is icy again. "Bye," she says to Adrian. To me, she doesn't even deign to say anything, which is fine.

Turning on her heel, she strides into the elevator.

As the doors close behind her, Adrian visibly relaxes. He steps up to the stroller, and when he sets his eyes on Piper, the expression on his face is borderline worshipful.

This time, I don't feel jealous of the baby. I'm glad she has so much love in her life.

Also, I'm very curious, so I tiptoe over and sneak a peek at her over Adrian's shoulder.

"Gorgeous, isn't she?" he whispers.

"Oh, I'll say." I grin at the chubby cheeks on display. "She's the kind of cute they use in diaper and baby formula commercials."

"I'm going to take her to the nursery," Adrian whispers and slowly pushes the stroller.

Just as we enter the nursery, Piper opens her eyes and starts fussing.

"It's okay," Adrian croons. "Daddy's right here."

I feel a pressure in my chest, and my eyes are suddenly watery.

Meanwhile, Adrian takes Piper out of the stroller and rocks her from side to side, whispering reassuring nothings to her.

If I'm ovulating, can I sue the makers of my IUD?

"Do you want to hold her?" Adrian offers in a way that reminds me of when Mary says she's willing to share the last of the chocolate ice cream.

"Just for a second," I say and gently take the baby.

Dash it all. She's so darn cute and smells so darn good. I already feel like I'm falling for her toothless charms. How crazy is that? The only other time I've felt this strongly toward a baby was when my sister was born.

It's like a part of my brain already sees her as family. Maybe it's because Adrian is my soon-to-be husband. Whatever passes for my spidey sense has gotten its signals crossed and doesn't realize this marriage isn't for real.

Adrian gets the milk out of the backpack, warms it, and brings it over.

Piper starts to fuss again.

"I think she wants you," I say.

And who can blame her, right?

"I think she wants the milk," Adrian says as he eagerly takes his daughter back.

With a tender smile, he kisses Piper's chubby little cheek—which soothes her immediately.

Again, can you blame her? Also, is it possible to overdose on adorableness?

He sits in the nearby rocker and puts the bottle to Piper's tiny lips.

Yep, adorableness overdose coming up—especially when he helps the little creature burp.

"Can you help me wash her?" Adrian says to me when the meal is over.

"Of course." The offer swells my chest with so much pride you'd think he's asked me to help him build a rocket to Mars.

When we get into the bathroom, Adrian removes his shirt.

Miss Miller doesn't usually abide foul language, but deuce take it! A gentleman ought not to put a lady's self-control to such a rigorous test.

I swallow an overabundance of saliva. Adrian's chiseled torso renders me speechless and unable to operate heavy machinery, which a baby bathtub hopefully isn't.

"I like to hold her skin to skin before the wash," he explains upon seeing some of my discomposure. "If you want to wait until—"

"No," I somehow manage to say. "It's totally fine." And by "fine," I mean my uterus is actively figuring out how to spit out the IUD.

Looking content, Adrian cradles Piper's little pink body to his hard chest.

It's official. I now truly understand the meaning of the terms "swoon" and "fit of the vapors." In fact, it takes considerable willpower not to succumb to both such conditions at once.

By the time Adrian is ready for the bath to begin, my knees feel wobbly and I'm forced to take a sharp breath to get myself together. For Piper to be safe, I must be on full alert.

The bath begins.

As it turns out, Adrian has a special fancy baby tub, one that will only dispense purified water that's a perfect ninety-nine degrees. This eases the process somewhat, as does the fact that Adrian is as good at this as he is at everything else.

Speaking of him being good, is this a bad time to ask him for my GD?

When Piper is dressed and lying in her crib, Adrian asks her if she wants to hear a story.

It could be my imagination, but I think she smiles in reply. Yep. She's definitely doing it. There's a flash of dimples and everything.

Adrian starts to read—and it becomes obvious that

this is a story he wrote just for her. A great story, in fact, and something she will surely enjoy even more when she's a little older. If she's anything like Mary was at this stage, he could read an accounting textbook to her and she'd enjoy it the same way as she does this.

Soon, Piper is fast asleep, so Adrian takes out his phone and mimes switching it to silent mode.

I do as he says, and he texts me.

I'm going to stay here for the rest of the night.

He nods at the nearby adult-sized bed before adding:

Feel free to go do your own thing.

What if my thing is to watch him sleep? Or sleep with him?

Blushing, I text him that I'll be exploring his library if he needs me, then leave.

Wow. If someone were to tell me Adrian spent a hundred million dollars to stock this library, I would not contradict that person. At first glance, I spot first editions of *The Last of the Mohicans, Ragged Dick, Little Women,* and *Grapes Of Wrath.*

Sadly, the selection of historical romance is negligently small. There are a few random classics by the biggest authors, including the *Bridgerton* series that he clearly bought after we met.

But hey. It's a start.

I leaf through one romance book that I don't recall reading. It sounds familiar, so I must have read it after all.

It's the one where the viscount discovers he's a bastard and thus cannot marry the heroine—even though he's impregnated her.

As I head over to start my evening routine, I keep dwelling on the idea of asking Adrian for my GD. This might be why, when I fall asleep, I dream of Adrian doing exactly that, which gets me pregnant despite my IUD. His sperm is that strong—one even waves its tail at me.

The resulting baby looks a lot like Piper, except she can speak from birth, and what she says is, "Just keep swimming," in the voice of Ellen DeGeneres.

"Does that mean I should name you Dori?" I ask her.

Before she can reply, my alarm wakes me up.

CHAPTER 26

Adrian

Piper's visit with me is over much, much too soon, and giving her back to Sydney in the afternoon is torture. I wish Jane were here, but she's at work.

As though sensing my mood, Leo clickety-clacks into the living room, leaps onto the couch, and cozies up to me.

"It will be much better after the hearing," I tell him. "Piper will spend half her time here."

Leo yawns.

Piper smells even better than bacon, and I don't make that comparison lightly.

I hug him and scratch behind his ears, which makes me feel somewhat better.

We hang out like that for a bit before I get a text from Jane.

Headed home soon. Want me to get anything on the way?

I look at Leo. "Want to go for a walk?"

Leo's eyes gleam excitedly. He jumps from the couch and sprints to the elevator.

I tell Jane that Leo and I will meet her on the way, and then I pack enough food for a small picnic, text an assistant to set up my favorite spot in the park, and head out.

As usual, Leo marks the first couple of trees like the fate of the world depends on it. From there, we walk briskly and catch Jane just as she's leaving the library.

"Hi," she says with a smile that lifts my mood and makes me want to kiss her sweetly curved lips.

Leo's tail wags so hard I half expect his butt to lift off the pavement, helicopter style.

"I've missed your yummy smell," Leo says to Jane.

She cocks her head. "Is that a hint? Should I use more deodorant?"

I grin. "Are you hungry?" I show her the basket.

"A picnic?!" she exclaims. "How very Victorian! I love that."

My mood improves further, and I offer her my arm. "Let's go. I know a great spot."

We walk leisurely, and Jane tells me about her day. When she asks about mine, I feel some of the earlier melancholy return. "The visit was too short," I say.

Jane squeezes my elbow. "You miss her terribly, don't you?"

I nod.

"Well, she's a special baby," Jane says. "I've just met

her, and I already miss her. In fact, if it weren't my second day at the new job, I would've totally stayed with you guys."

"Don't even worry about it," I say. "But since you've brought up how busy you are with the new job, I wanted to ask you... Do you think you could get away for an hour during lunch?"

"I think so," she says. "To go where?"

"City Hall," I say. "To get a marriage license, the couple is required to be there in person."

She lets go of my arm and stares at me, eyes wide. "Is it time for that already?"

"This is just to get the license, which is valid for sixty days," I explain. "That way, we have a largish window to actually tie the knot."

She looks overwhelmed. "When do you want to do that bit?"

"I'm thinking sooner rather than later," I say soothingly. "Just waiting on advice from my lawyers and the PR firm."

She rolls her eyes. "How romantic."

The word "romantic"—or was it "how?"—triggers something in Leo's doggy brain, and he rips at the leash with all his might, causing it to slip out of my grip.

"Oh, no!" Jane exclaims. "Someone is about to get pushed into the mud!"

Fuck. Not that. I already have a wife candidate; I don't need Leo to choose me another.

I start running, but Leo speeds up.

"Stop!" I yell. "Sit!"

The dog either doesn't hear me or ignores the commands.

Maybe I should invest in those inhumane-seeming dog collars that have spikes? No way. But I *could* hire a team of dog catchers—assuming that's a thing—so that they could walk nearby to intercept Leo when he does this.

At least he's headed toward my chosen picnic spot, just much faster than is reasonable.

"Where is he going?" Jane pants from about a foot away.

Huh. She's kept up with us? "I have no idea," I reply over my shoulder.

Soon, though, I get an inkling, and I don't like it one bit.

There's a lady walking a King Poodle female in the distance. At least, I presume she's female based on the dog's pink collar and even pinker bow. The bitch—I mean the dog, of course—has recently received one of those signature pompadour haircuts that exposes the butt, and I strongly suspect said rear end is Leo's destination. Not that I'm saying a female with her butt exposed is "asking for it" or anything like that. Besides, Leo is probably drawn to her smell, not the look.

"Leo, down!" I yell.

Nope.

He reaches the female, ignores the loud protestations of the human lady, and takes a good inhale of pedigreed poodle ass.

"Help!" the lady shouts.

I speed up because the poodle seems to be "flagging" Leo her interest—at least I assume that's why she's so pointedly showcasing her butt to him.

Just as Leo gets ready to mount, I arrive on the scene, grab his leash, and pull him away.

Leo gives me a betrayed look that seems to say, "Dude, cockblock much?"

The poodle glares at me too, and the meaning of her gaze is pretty much the same as that of Leo, but in French.

The human female clutches her pearls—yes, she's wearing them—and is screaming things like, "Atrocity," and "Diseased mutt," and "I'll neuter him myself!"

"No one is neutering anyone," I say firmly. "Leo is very sorry, and so am I."

Leo does look sorry... that I got there in time to stop him.

"Sorry?" the lady shouts. "He almost raped my Sisi."

I look at Jane for help. The last thing I want to do as a guy is make excuses when it comes to sexual consent, even if we're talking about dogs.

Jane peers at the poodle. "I think she's in heat."

"How dare you?" the lady snaps.

"See how her tail is curled to the side?" Jane points at the appendage in question. "Before she was fixed, that would happen to Lassie too." Turning to me, Jane adds, "She was the dog we had when I was a kid."

"Her tail does that from time to time," the lady says, sounding unsure. "When she's on her period."

"One that comes every six months or so?" Jane asks.

Frowning, the lady nods.

"Is Sisi fixed?" Jane continues.

The lady lifts her chin. "She's beyond such things."

I can tell Jane is having a hard time keeping her face calm. "Even if Sisi is beyond such things, she is in heat, which means her pheromones will have an effect on the male dogs she comes into contact with."

The lady pulls on Sisi's leash. "I will not stand here and continue this vulgar conversation." With that, she struts away, with Sisi turning around from time to time to cast longing looks at Leo—though that last bit could just be my imagination.

Leo whines.

For the love of naked butts, just one sniff, please. Pretty please.

"Sorry, bud," I say. "Maybe peanut butter will make you feel better?"

The whining stops.

I grin. "If the devil ever wanted the souls of dogs, Leo's would cost him a jar of peanut butter."

Jane grins back. "Most other dogs' too."

I gesture at my favorite picnic spot. "What do you think?"

Jane examines it. "Isn't someone already sitting there?"

"Yeah. Us," I say. "I had my assistant set it up."

Jane hurries over to the blanket with evident excitement, while I walk over to the pole in the ground and attach Leo's leash to it thoroughly—I don't want to chase him again.

Once Leo is secure, I give him his favorite hollowed-out butt-plug-looking toy that has frozen peanut butter inside.

"Now everyone has something to munch on," I say to Jane, then open the basket and pull out the food for us humans.

"Cucumber sandwiches?" Jane exclaims. "Do you have tea too?"

"What am I, a barbarian?" Pulling out a thermos, I pour each of us a cup.

When Jane tastes hers, the blissful expression on her face does to me what poodle pheromones must've done to Leo—except I have more self-control.

I think.

"Are there spices in this tea?" Jane asks, licking her lips. "Like in chai?"

I shake my head, trying not to think about what I'd like that tongue to lick instead.

"What about molasses?"

"Nope." My voice is slightly hoarse.

"What kind of tea is it then?"

I strain to recall. "Da Hong Pao, I think."

"I think it's now my favorite," she says. "I've never had tea that smelled like an orchid before."

"It's a good tea," I say, finally asserting my control over Yoda. And to keep said control, I add, "I also have a tea that is fertilized by the dung of panda bears—but I figured I'd warn you before brewing something like that."

There. Dung is unsexy, and pandas refuse to propagate their species—also a mood killer.

Jane's nose crinkles. "Why would you use that as fertilizer?"

I shrug. "Something about the bears only digesting thirty percent of the nutrients in wild bamboo. Or maybe it's a marketing ploy."

"A weird one," Jane says, then darts a glance at Leo and blushes.

I check what the problem is.

Done with his treat, Leo has decided to give a certain part of his anatomy a tongue bath to work off the tension from his unconsummated encounter.

I clear my throat. "I hope you don't mind," I say to Jane. "I don't want to shame him for doing that."

"It's fine," Jane says, keeping her gaze on anything but Leo's tongue. "He's only doing what all men fantasize about."

I can't help myself. "My fantasies involve others."

As I could've predicted, her blush deepens. "Has Leo ever actually had sex?" Jane asks in a clear attempt to change the subject.

I shake my head, Yoda back in action. Not at the thought of Leo having sex, of course, but of a certain small, cute female of the human species doing so.

"Then why is he intact?" Jane presses.

Okay, that topic is also a mood killer, thankfully.

"You've never done it either, yet no one is suggesting you get fixed, right?"

Impossibly, her cheeks turn another shade redder. "I think when Mom talked me into getting my IUD, the sentiment was similar to that of dog owners."

I chuckle. "I know it's silly, but I've always pictured myself under the knife and decided I couldn't do it to Leo. After today, though, I might consider having him get a vasectomy."

Jane cocks her head. "No sheep-like puppies for him?"

"No." I scratch my head. "I'm not even sure if he'll ever get to have sex. I always figured that unless I had a female dog always available for him, letting him try sex would just make him miserable for the majority of the time when it's not available."

"Oh?" Jane says. "Is that your self-enforced celibacy talking?"

"Maybe." I sigh. "But still, one can't miss what one has never tried."

Jane's cheeks reach the infrared zone once again. "I think one *can* miss it without trying it."

She has a point. When I was a teen, I was dying to have sex long before any girl was willing to do it with me. Also, we're back on the topic we really shouldn't be on... because Yoda.

"I guess I'll have to find Leo some willing female dog as a girlfriend," I say, trying to get back to the canines. "I'm sure there are agencies and such that can help me out."

"Right," Jane says tentatively. "And since we're on the subject of devirginization, I've been wanting to ask you for a big favor..."

No.

There's no way she—

"Adrian," she says, looking down and blushing even more fiercely. "Would you Grandly Deflower me?"

CHAPTER 27

Jane

I. Can't. Believe. I. Just. Asked. Him. That.

I blame the picnic, the most romantic activity ever invented. Oh, and the earlier running—it got my heart pumping and my brain must've gotten oxygen deprived.

Even the heavenly tea is complicit.

And the—

Wait a second. Why hasn't Adrian responded?

By Jove! A proper gentleman would go deaf—or at least pretend to—rather than acknowledge that Miss Miller would make such an unseemly query.

Feeling like my heart is falling through my stomach, I raise my eyes to meet Adrian's gaze.

Nope. He has heard me *and* understood. He's just thinking of a reply.

Why are we not in Florida? A sinkhole in the ground would be very welcome right about now.

Just as I debate cooling my cheeks with the cucumber

slices from one of the sandwiches—or maybe stuffing the whole thing down my throat so I choke and die—Adrian finally opens his mouth.

"I'm very honored," he says huskily. "Having said that... I don't think it's a good idea."

His words are like a round kick into the gut.

I somehow find myself on my feet.

"Wait," Adrian says.

I do not. Instead, I'm running. I don't know where, and I don't know why.

As I approach the nearby lake, a hand grabs my shoulder.

I twist around. "Don't touch me!"

"Sorry," Adrian says, looking with great concern at something behind me. "Please. Don't do anything rash."

My hammering heart nearly stops as I follow his gaze... to a boat rental.

Huh? "You think I plan to go into the lake? Why? Because you think so highly of yourself?"

He takes a step back. "Highly of myself? What do you mean?"

I roll my eyes. "You think you're *so* special that a rejection from you would make me want to drown myself in the nearest body of water? Should I avoid roofs too?"

He sighs deeply. "I merely thought... The lake is a place I can't follow you."

Ah. Right. He's got issues with water. "I wasn't even thinking of going near it."

"Good," he says.

Does the relief on his face mean he cares about what happens to me?

Nah. He's just glad he won't have to seek another fake wife candidate after I drown.

"I want to be alone," I say. "I shouldn't need to go to the lake to accomplish that."

"Look, I said I'm sorry," he says. "I didn't set out to hurt your feelings. I just don't want to jeopardize our arrangement. Nor do I feel worthy of doing what you asked."

"You've got that last one right," I say. "You're *not* worthy."

There. I turn around and flee again, and this time, he doesn't follow.

He calls me instead, which I let go to voicemail.

He texts something too, but I don't read it.

I'm still fuming that he said no.

Does he not understand that asking him was the bravest moment of my life?

Then again, maybe I shouldn't have asked him.

It does carry a risk of messing up things between us.

Hell, we haven't even done anything, and things are tense.

As I walk, I feel enough embarrassment to kill a blobfish. Relatedly, I also feel *like* a blobfish, or an anglerfish—or something else that lives in the darkest depths of the ocean, and therefore can look as hideous as she wants.

My phone rings.

He's persistent, isn't he?

I reach to send the call to voicemail when I see that it's my mom who is calling.

Hesitating for a moment, I pick up.

"Hello," I say.

"What happened?" Mom asks, sounding worried.

Damn, she's good. "What do you mean?"

"You sound upset," she says.

"Do I?" I ask, forcing joviality into my voice.

"Yes," Mom says. "Like that time when that idiot never picked you up for prom."

Fine. She's been filling the role of my best friend for many years now, so I tell her what happened, even if I feel more embarrassed in the process.

"That's a conundrum," Mom says when I finish.

"A conundrum?"

She sighs. "Many ways of looking at the thing is what I mean."

"Like?"

"For starters, it's not cool to be so mean to someone for not wanting to have sex with you. When men do it to me, I hate it."

"I didn't just ask him to have sex," I say, offended. "Also, how am I being mean?"

"You're refusing his calls," she says. "And since you're instrumental in his plans for his daughter, he's probably worried sick."

Shit. I hate it when Mom has a good point.

"I'll text him back right after this," I say. "And you'd better have other ways of looking at this so-called conundrum."

"The part where he said he doesn't feel worthy," she says. "That's something that only someone who *is* worthy would say... before he's sure about his feelings for you."

I get another text from Adrian, which adds to the guilt Mom has kindled in me.

"That last bit makes no sense," I tell Mom. "But I'd better go."

"Don't forget about the money that's on the line," Mom shouts before I can hang up.

Great. Now, as I reply, I'll feel like I'm doing so for the money.

Regardless, I hit reply to his last message:

Can we pretend I never asked anything?

He responds immediately:

Asked what?

With a sigh, I text him that I'll see him at home.

Miss Miller would notify the gentleman that she's ready to accept a properly worded apology.

Then again, based on my talk with Mom, I'm not sure if I shouldn't be the one to apologize.

Not that that would ever happen.

I'd rather lose out on all those millions.

A new text arrives, and it's from Mom—though, given what she says, I wish the so-called advice it contains were coming from someone else. Anyone else, except possibly Mary.

Dress slutty around the house, is Mom's pearl of mature wisdom. *It will make him regret his choice—and possibly change his mind.*

Do other people's moms ever give such advice? Somehow, I doubt it. Maybe not even friends their own age.

The biggest problem with Mom's idea is that Adrian might not care if I pranced around his place completely naked. Clearly, I'm a sexless prop to him, something he can present at court. Something that screams "I'm so not into sleeping around that I married an unfuckable wife... just look at her."

Still. It's not like I have anything to lose. In fact, he wanted to see my Victorian cosplay. It wouldn't take that much effort to turn a lady's outfit into that of a courtesan.

Yeah. It will be a bit like Halloween, when my fellow females make all sorts of costumes sexy, from nurses to skunks.

My mood lifts as I keep thinking in this direction. When not in cosplay, I could wear those shorts that I deemed too small and tight a few years back—which is when my rearend decided to have a growth spurt. I've also got plenty of cute sports bras and hot yoga pants that I could use.

Also, I could go shopping. After all, I've got a job now, and I'm about to become a millionaire.

Thus decided, I take an Uber to Forever 21 and shop for sexy outfits. I even get some lacy lingerie, in case I feel bold enough to "accidentally" bump into Adrian while wearing it to, say, the kitchen at night.

This may be an uncharitable thought, but Miss Miller

wouldn't consider some of these so-called undergarments befitting a woman of even the loosest morals.

The good news is that I feel almost happy when I'm done with the spree. Is this why women find this activity so fun? Until now, I only found shopping fun when it took place at bookstores.

Loaded with bags, I return to Adrian's place, where Leo meets me and sniffs all my bags as though whatever I bought were obviously for him. As I head to my room to put the stuff down, Leo keeps sniffing me.

Oh, well. I guess I'm changing into my slutty Victorian lady outfit in front of the dog.

It takes a while, yet Leo watches me like I'm a TV show he's binging.

"Where's your dad?" I ask him when my evil outfit is complete.

No reaction.

"Adrian," I say to the dog. "Is he home?"

At the sound of his human's name, Leo's ears become animated. He trots out of my room, and I follow him to the gym.

"Hey," I say as I step inside... and then I gape at the view on display, my mouth watering—along with other, more unmentionable places.

Wearing only shorts, Adrian is doing pull-ups.

As his back muscles defy gravity, they flex and harden —and the visage is so arousing I debate bolting to my room so that I can play my pink violin. Before I can do that, though, Leo barks.

Adrian finishes his pull-up and turns.

Oh, my. He looks even more ravishing from the front —and he's totally, unequivocally beating me at my own game, a game he didn't even know he was playing.

There are beads of sweat rolling down his torso that I want to lick, and if one wanted to study anatomy, his glistening muscles would be the perfect tool.

At the risk of sounding dull and unadventurous, Miss Miller would dare say this whole situation is the very definition of inappropriate.

"Hi," Adrian says, and even his voice is extra yummy for some reason, husky and reminiscent of To'ak chocolate.

"Hello," I reply, stumbling over all those syllables. "Was the weather nice on your way home from the picnic?"

"Yeah. It was nice and warm. I saw a couple of clouds. One was shaped like a Vitruvian man." He scans me from head to foot. "Is this one of the Victorian outfits you mentioned?"

I nod.

He cocks his head. "They didn't have anything like it on *Bridgerton*."

Right, but they did have something like it on another show.

Harlots.

CHAPTER 28
Adrian

I don't know what they call any of the clothing items Jane has on, but I want to rip each and every one of them into little shreds, then do to her exactly what she suggested a few hours ago.

But I can't.

Shouldn't.

I had good reasons when I declined, and if Yoda ever lets the blood return to my brain, I'm sure I'll remember what those reasons were.

"Speaking of *Bridgerton*," Jane says. "We should watch it later."

I hope this means she isn't mad at me any longer. Then again, she likes that show enough to watch it with Hitler. Either way, I agree. Then, very casually, I ask, "Will you still be wearing that outfit when we do?"

If so, I'd better pregame Yoda and take a cold shower, just in case.

Is that a smirk on Jane's face when she considers my question?

Nah. That would make no sense.

Finally, she shakes her head. "This outfit is too starchy to walk in, let alone sit on a couch in."

Thank the Force, Yoda will.

"I dressed this way because I wanted to make that extra million dollars," Jane adds, sounding oddly guilty.

"You'll get your money," I reassure her. It will be well spent because it's not every day you get a paradigm shift. Until this moment, I didn't think Victorian women could possibly have been sexy. On top of being prim and prudish, they didn't have showers and covered every inch of their bodies. Now, though, I wish Jane and I could do some roleplaying, with her as a lady and me a—

"Okay," Jane says. "Get back to your workout."

With a shrug, I do, though I see in the mirror that she doesn't leave—probably because she wants to know how to use all the equipment when it comes time for her to exercise. To that end, I know the polite thing would be to offer to work out together, but I don't think I'll manage that without a serious case of blue balls.

So I work my back as I usually would, then triceps, and just as I finish the last set, Jane sneaks out.

Hmm. I look at Leo, who wakes up from his twentieth nap of the day.

"Did Jane think I didn't know she was there the whole time?" I ask him.

Leo cocks his head.

Humans overcomplicate things. Pretend she's a poodle in heat and just mount her. Smooth as non-crunchy peanut butter.

I head into the shower and do some Yoda Yoga on the off-chance Jane forgets to change. And boy, am I glad that I took that precaution because when I meet Jane in the living room, she's wearing an outfit that's even hotter than the last, with lots of very lickable pale skin exposed.

"I changed," she says when she notices me staring at her. "As you requested."

Not exactly as I requested, but it's not like I can tell her that.

"Let's watch," I say and plop on the couch.

She sits next to me, and we start to Netflix—with me being anything but chill. In fact, being with Jane like this is very hard—in many senses of the word. I can't wait until the show is over so I can have some alone time with Yoda. Again.

"What do you think?" Jane asks when the credits roll on season two.

"I think I know why Victorians had all those strict sex-related rules."

Shit. Bad topic.

"Religion?" Jane asks, focusing all her attention on me.

I shake my head. "Lack of internet and therefore porn."

Oops. Seriously, I usually have more of a filter between my mouth and my brain.

Jane narrows her eyes slightly and styles her left eyebrow into a question mark.

"Without porn, there would've been less masturbation," I explain, because I'm committed to this now. "Without masturbation, people got that much hornier. Hence men going crazy upon seeing a flash of an ankle."

Speaking of ankles, Jane's are extremely dainty and pretty, making me wonder if kissing them would—

"Few people really used the internet before the early nineties," Jane counters. "Yet there was all that free love business in the sixties."

"Sure, but there was porn by then," I say, sounding less sure of myself. "On tapes, or as pictures before that."

"They had porn as pictures in Victorian times," Jane says triumphantly. "So there goes your theory."

Hmm. Didn't they have to pose for hours for pictures back then? I bet the poor girls would get cold sitting naked for that long. Still, Jane's got a point. Seems like masturbation isn't the key to *everything*, even if it seems to be at the moment.

Clouding my judgement, Yoda is.

Jane stands up, treating me to a view of her shapely legs. "Good night."

With that, she sashays away, leaving me to sit and wait until Yoda calms down enough for me to be able to walk.

The next day, I pick up Jane to go to City Hall. The whole time, all she talks to me about is the weather. So much for my hope that she was no longer mad about my refusal of her generous offer.

To be honest, I'm mad at myself too. Maybe we could make it work somehow. Maybe the risk isn't so great.

No.

Must stay strong.

Besides, Jane likely felt insulted, so she's unlikely to give me another chance at her GD.

To prove that last point, on the way back, the weather is still the main topic.

To test the waters, I say, "The forecast is particularly nice for tomorrow. Would you like to have another picnic?"

She purses her lips. "Big day at the library. I doubt I'll be able to get away."

Translation: she's definitely still mad at me. Judging by her reaction the last time, picnics are her catnip.

"Fair enough," I say. Before we can get back to discussing wind speeds, humidity, or the UV index, I add, "I've settled on a date for the wedding." In truth, I haven't heard from my people yet, but I want to seal the deal before Jane decides she is so upset about the GD refusal that she wants to back out.

"Oh," Jane says without any enthusiasm. "When is the big day?"

"The first Saturday of next month," I say, figuring that's the soonest the event organizer can put a wedding together. "Is that going to be enough time for you to invite whoever you want to be at the ceremony?"

She frowns. "Do I have to invite anyone?"

"I guess not, but this is supposed to look like a real wedding."

She sighs. "You're right. Besides, Grandma would not forgive me if she didn't get an invite."

"We have a planner," I say. "She'll take care of things like invites. Just email me the names and addresses of your peeps."

Jane pulls up her phone, compiles a list, and sends it to me. I pass it on to the planner and try to strike up a real conversation with Jane, only to end up talking about the weather again.

When Jane comes home that night, she changes into yoga pants and a sports bra that drive me insane, so I'm almost glad when she tells me she doesn't want to watch TV together. It would have been exquisite torture if she'd said yes.

Still, her refusal proves beyond a shadow of doubt that she's upset with me—and only joined me last night because we still had *Bridgerton* season two to finish. Now that that's over, she's too pissed at me to watch anything else.

Hmm. I wonder how much it would cost to pay Netflix to speed up the shooting of the next season. Jane wouldn't be able to resist *that...*

I look it up. They paid seven million per episode. I could afford that. Then again...

A germline of an idea springs to life.

What if I made my own show, one a lot like *Bridgerton*? Better yet, why not make it a movie? There aren't a lot of very good historical romance films on the market. If it does well, it could always be spun off into a show. More importantly, Jane wouldn't be able to resist talking about it with me.

Excited, I go to my studio and start my research.

By the following day, my relationship with Jane still hasn't improved. She doesn't want to spend time with me, though she is wearing another Victorian outfit that drives me insane.

Speaking of Victorian things, since my *Bridgerton* knock-off movie is in its infant stage, I don't mention it to her just yet. I have a lot more work to do before it's anything worth discussing. In fact, now that I've started, a part of me wants to keep it a secret, and just show her the finished product when I'm done. Either way, the movie is what I focus on over the next week, given that Jane is determined to avoid me.

She's clearly still upset with me. However, we do have snippets of conversation here and there, and when Piper comes over, Jane does spend time with us—which makes me regret my GD refusal all the more.

She wasn't bragging when she said she's good with babies.

"You sweet little thing," she coos, rocking Piper back and forth as my daughter grabs her hair with her chubby little fist. "Let's burp you and make you feel better, why don't we?"

And as I watch in amazement, my fussy baby smiles at her angelically and lets out a very ladylike burp, somehow keeping down all of her milk in the process.

Seriously, is Jane a baby whisperer or what?

Piper either refuses to burp with me properly, or I get thrown up on half the time.

"You need to teach me how to do that," I say as Jane hands my daughter—fed, burped, and changed—back to me. "There's a trick to this, right?"

She grins. "Yes, and it's having a much younger sister and a mom who insists you babysit. Here, let me show you."

She demonstrates her technique on a teddy bear, and I imprint it into my memory—as I do everything Jane-related these days. I simply can't get her off my mind, and not just because by the week before the wedding, Yoda is ready to join the dark side of the Force thanks to her outfits, which are ridiculously sexy even when they're not Victorian.

Aren't librarians supposed to dress all boring? Because mine does not.

My new project doesn't help. In order to better understand the historical romance genre, I've purchased a bunch of books that Jane likes and have been binge-reading them. Turns out, these books are chockfull of sexy scenes, most of which feature a virginal heroine.

Yes. That's right.

I refused to partake in a GD, and now I'm reading all about them—an activity that has a similar effect on me as reading cookbooks would on a starving man.

CHAPTER 29

Jane

Hell is sometimes depicted as a place where your desires go unfulfilled. For example, gluttons are surrounded by delicious food that they can't eat, or drunkards are swimming in liquor they can't consume. Now, I'm not a sex addict, far from it, but the weeks before the wedding make me feel like one... in my particular version of hell.

Apparently, working out isn't the only thing Adrian does shirtless. He doesn't wear a shirt when he goes to the fridge at night, or when he sunbathes on his rooftop deck, or when he plays in the ball pit with Leo. And let's not forget his shirtless skin-to-skin with Piper, of course.

That last one is why I'm beginning to forget the sting of his rejection. The more time I spend with the baby, the more I fall for her, and that makes me think that Adrian was right to say no to my GD proposal.

This whole marriage is for Piper's sake, and I almost messed it up, even with him saying no.

As we get closer to the wedding, I don't even have time to think about my GD. When I'm not working, most of my time is spent choosing a dress and liaising with the wedding planner (who seems to defer to the opinion of the bride on pretty much everything).

Before I know it, the wedding day arrives. As I get my hair, nails, and makeup professionally done, butterflies come to life in my stomach, and by the time I'm putting on my wedding dress, I have a major case of the jitters... as though I were a real bride.

Which I'm not.

I have to keep reminding myself of that as I put in my contacts—something I only do on special occasions.

I'm so busy doing that I don't even notice when Mom, Mary, and Grandma join me in the fitting room. I only realize they're there when all three of them start sobbing.

"Who died?" I demand.

"You just look so beautiful," Mary says, sniffling. "Like a princess."

"You're not my little baby anymore," Mom mutters over a hiccup.

"And I'm a social crier," Grandma says, blowing her nose. "Always have been."

"Can I go?" I ask Mrs. Dubois and the rest of the glam-me-up team.

Mrs. Dubois looks me over with her super-critical eye and nods, albeit grudgingly. "I still wish I had six months," she says, her French accent in full force. "But given the current constraints, you look decent enough."

Mary huffs. "Especially if by 'decent,' you mean 'Disney princess-like.'"

"Or 'queen-like,'" Mom adds.

I resist the urge to point out that it was, in fact, Queen Victoria who put the now-familiar white dress on the map for the countless brides who followed her.

The door opens and the event organizer rushes in, looking panicked—though that seems to be her default state of being. "The limo is here," she rattles out. "We need the bride at the church. Stat."

"Fucking amateurs," Mrs. Dubois mutters under her breath. Noticing my grandma's chastising glare, she adds, "Pardon my French."

I let myself be herded into the limo, and when the car is en route, Mom asks, "Why St. George's Church? I don't think it's the biggest or most architecturally significant."

I grin. "If today's wedding had a theme, it would be 'historical romance.'"

"I still don't get it," Mom says.

I roll my eyes. "If you'd read the books I've been recommending, you'd notice that all the fashionable weddings of the ton took place at St. George's."

"But in London," Mom says.

I shrug. "I figured this St. George's would be easier to book on short notice. Or did you want to fly today?"

Mom shakes her head. "Whatever makes you happy."

"Actually, a quick, nondescript wedding would make me happy," I say. "The kind they have in Vegas or at City Hall."

"If you did that, you wouldn't be able to do a historical romance theme," Mom says.

I purse my lips. "We could've roleplayed. In my romances, they have quick weddings all the time. If the heroine is preggers, for example, the hero just gets a Special License from the Archbishop of Canterbury."

I've done some research on this, and in the real world, said license was granted infrequently and not lightly—in contrast to my books, where getting the license isn't all that special.

"So it's the groom who wants it to be fancy?" Grandma asks. "That's not how it worked in my day."

"Jane does too," Mary says conspiratorially. "She just wants us to think she's above such things."

The limo stops at that moment, which is good, because I don't have a witty retort to that statement.

"Don't leave the car," I tell everyone as they reach for the doors. "We need to wait for security."

"Security?" Grandma looks out the window, her expression concerned.

I sigh. "The tabloids are interested in our... I mean, Adrian's wedding. There will be paparazzi outside the church and the hotel where the reception will take place."

"Oh." Grandma grins. "How exciting."

I'm not excited at all. I'm not sure why, but I feel icky knowing that Adrian actually wants those photos so that the whole world knows about the wedding. The security is just for appearances' sake. The paparazzi will still snap a bunch of photos of the both of us. In fact, the last time

Adrian and I had a tête-à-tête unrelated to the weather, he told me that his security team discovered that some so-called journalists have infiltrated the catering staff and will pose as waiters and the like so that they can later report on the wedding.

The limo door opens, and I'm blinded by the flashes of the cameras as the security team ushers us down a red carpet and into the church.

Someone covers my face with a veil, so my visibility becomes limited.

"I'll walk you," Mom says solemnly, as if reading my mind.

We walk into the church's main hall. The place is packed to the brim, but the guests are hard to discern behind the veil, though I think I recognize the city mayor, a few famous actors, and even the billionaire who was in the newspapers recently because he plans to take a trip to the moon.

Yep. This is the modern version of the ton.

A live orchestra starts playing "Here Comes the Bride."

My heartbeat skyrockets.

The official name of this tune is "Bridal Chorus," and it's from an opera called *Lohengrin* by Richard Wagner (who had the dubious honor of being one of Hitler's favorite composers). It was played during the wedding of Queen Victoria's daughter (also Victoria) and has been associated with weddings ever since—despite the fact that, in the opera, it was sung as the couple entered the bridal chamber, not as the bride (Elsa—

without any snow-related powers) walked down the aisle. It's also worth mentioning that in said opera, when separated from her new husband, Elsa dies of grief.

So, yeah. I'm not sure why everyone uses this tune given the associations, but in my case, it does seem fitting.

I know ahead of time that Adrian and I will get divorced, so I'd better shield my heart lest I end up like poor Elsa.

CHAPTER 30
Adrian

Fuck me. Even with the veil obscuring her features, Jane is beautifully radiant as she majestically floats down the aisle.

My breathing speeds up—and I have to remind myself for the umpteenth time that this isn't real.

It's just a show for the upcoming hearing.

My emotions are just mixed up because of how realistic this all seems.

Click.

There. That was someone snapping a picture—probably one of the paparazzi who thinks it was their stealth that helped them infiltrate this wedding, not my security team turning a blind eye.

I glance to my right, where my best-in-the-world security guard/nanny is holding Piper, her broad back blocking the pictures as I instructed her to do.

Jane and I have no choice but to end up in the tabloids, but my daughter's privacy will not be violated.

I turn back to Jane just as she reaches me, and I can see that she looks overwhelmed, which makes me want to cancel this whole thing and give her a huge hug instead.

But no.

The show must go on.

"Dearly beloved," says the priest. Or is he a bishop? "We are gathered today—"

Jane lifts her veil, and seeing her feels like a sunrise during a vampire apocalypse.

The bishop continues his spiel. I only half listen until we get to the vows part, and he makes Jane say something that I presume she herself picked out from her Victorian repertoire.

Among other things, Jane promises to "obey me," which sounds vaguely BDSM-y.

Like it, Yoda does.

"You may kiss the bride," the bishop finally says.

I lay my hand on Jane's lower back and pull her to me, the scent of guava with a subtle hint of begonia making my head spin.

As we look deeply into each other's eyes, hers gleam —and the cameras begin to click just as I dip my head and claim her mouth.

The church seems to disappear. Jane's lips are soft, pliant, and taste like strawberries. She's also returning the kiss with unvirginal eagerness, which might be why I deepen it, invading her mouth with my tongue in the way I'd like to do with my—

The bishop angrily clears his throat.

Cockblocker.

As I pull away from Jane, the crowd in the church goes wild, clapping, cheering, and whistling.

Between this kiss and the legendary honeymoon suite we have booked at the hotel, no one will have any doubt that Jane and I are going to consummate this marriage.

But, of course, we will not. I have to remind myself (and Yoda) of that.

"The carriage is ready," the security guard holding Piper loudly whispers.

I kiss my daughter, wave at Jane's family, then take my new wife by the hand and lead her down the aisle.

People pelt us with rose petals as we go. Isn't it supposed to be rice? Must be some historical romance thing—as is the horse-drawn carriage outside with a bunch of old pots and pans attached to the rear bumper.

"Will you keep an eye on Piper?" I ask my new mother-in-law before she follows the baby and her bodyguard into the limo.

"It will be my pleasure," she says with a wide grin. "Enjoy the ride."

I smile at Jane. "How does it feel to be Mrs. Westfield?"

Jane moistens her kiss-swollen lips, but before she utters her reply, the carriage begins to move, creating a horrible noise that could deafen a corpse.

"I'm sorry," Jane shouts over the clamor. "The pans sounded like a good idea when I read about them in my books." Or at least, I think that's what she says.

We proceed forward, and plenty of people look up at us and take a picture—which is an unforeseen benefit of the noise. The cacophony has another advantage too. It tempers some of the emotions stirred up by that much-too-real kiss. I need that, to be calmer, if I'm to survive the first dance and the rest of the activities we have planned.

After what feels like an hour of ear torture, we finally stop.

"Wow," Jane says. "You weren't kidding. This place fits the theme perfectly."

I proudly puff out my chest. The Palace Hotel was one of my few contributions to the wedding plans. I did some research, and it came up on a list of locations where an actual royal wedding has taken place.

Oh, and the best part is that it looks as the name would imply—like a palace.

When we enter the lobby, Jane spots the porters and grins. I smile too. The guys are wearing cosplay-style costumes that include capes, bicorns, and bright pantaloons.

"If I were the owner, I would've stopped at the parrots," I whisper to Jane as I take in the birds filling the lobby. "The peacocks are a bit of a cliché."

"I love it all," she says, gawking at one of said peacocks. "This is the closest you can get to having a fairytale wedding."

I'm glad she thinks so. Booking this place wasn't just a matter of money. You have to request the Palace far in advance, which I didn't, so I had to entice the couple who held today's slot with a wedding at The Pikaia Lodge in Ecuador.

"Mr. Westfield?" asks one of the bicorn-clad dudes.

I nod.

The guy lifts a walkie-talkie to summon Kevin, the photographer I hired.

Jane chuckles when she spots Kevin, and I smile as well. Kevin seems to have taken the wedding theme a little bit too close to the heart because he's dressed like some sort of a duke, and even holds a quizzing glass to his eye when he examines us plebeians.

I assume Kevin grudgingly approves of what he sees because he waves for us to follow him.

When we enter the giant room where the photoshoot is to take place, everyone who has the honor of being in the wedding album is already waiting for us—including Leo, who's standing next to his new (male) dog walker.

Spotting the big green screen in the back, Jane looks askance at me.

"So we can create any background we want," I explain. "Don't worry, it will look so realistic everyone will think we were at that location."

"Can one of them be Hyde Park?" Jane asks. Glancing at the rest of our posse, she explains, "That's where the members of the British aristocracy would typically hang out in Victorian times."

Kevin glares at Jane haughtily through his quizzing glass. "'Any' background obviously includes Hyde Park and every other park."

I angrily clear my throat. "Kevin, you're not actually a duke."

Looking sheepish, the photographer pockets his

quizzing glass and grabs the camera. In a much more respectful tone, he says, "Why don't we start with the family of the bride?"

Jane's grandmother—what was her name?—and her sister, Mary, rush over to where Kevin points. Jane's mother, Georgiana, walks up to me, with Piper's security guard on her tail. With great reluctance, Georgiana places Piper back into my arms.

"I feel like she's part of our family already," she says with a sigh.

I hold Piper to my chest and feel a rollercoaster of warring emotions. Love and contentment win the mix—because I feel them so strongly anytime I'm in my daughter's presence. But there are notes of longing and jealousy in my chest too because Jane has this whole family with her, and Piper is the only member of mine.

"She can be in the pictures with you," I say and force myself to offer Piper back.

Beaming with happiness, Georgiana grabs the baby and reunites with Jane's peeps.

Leo drags his new overseer over, then reassuringly sticks his wet nose into the palm of my hand.

You don't just have Piper. You've got me too.

Smiling, I pet my sheep-like best friend. Speaking of friends, Bernard, Warren, and Michael are walking my way.

Instantly, my self-pity party is over. The other kids at the prep school called our group The Four Musketeers, and it fits because we got into as many scrapes as the famous Dumas' characters.

"I can't believe you're getting your balls shackled," Michael says in a voice low enough so only the four of us can hear him.

"And voluntarily too," Bernard adds.

"And where did she find shackles that tiny?" Michael continues.

"I suspect she's got something on him," Warren says to the others with mock concern.

"Oh, shit," Bernard says to me conspiratorially. "Blink twice if she's got a bomb in your butthole."

"Or any other hole," Michael adds.

"You're a hole," I say. "All three of you are."

"That's the weakest burn in the history of burns," Michael says.

Do other grown men de-evolve back to their teenage selves when they get together like this, no matter how many years have passed? Anyone who knows these three as they are now would not believe the words coming out of their highly respected mouths.

"Wait a second," Michael says with a grin. "Is she the sex bot you always wanted to invent?"

"Why would he marry his sex bot?" Warren asks. "The beauty of a sex bot is that you don't need a wife. Or a girlfriend."

"Enough," Barnard says. In a more serious tone, he asks me, "Are you having cold feet at all?"

"Cold feet?" Michael exclaims. "No way! I bet he invented some special shoe warmers just for that, and is wearing them now."

I tune out the rest of the ribbing and watch the

photo shoot until Kevin asks the four of us to step up to the green screen.

"Do not fuck around during the shoot," I say to my friends in a tone that hopefully conveys my ability—and eagerness—to kick the guilty party in the balls.

They either get the message or remember who they actually are and behave with dignity as the shoot starts.

The only problem is their smiles are fake, but who cares, right?

Suddenly, Leo rips at his leash, frees himself from the new walker, and beelines for Kevin's crotch.

Since hurt balls are still at the forefront of my mind, I cringe.

Only Leo isn't interested in causing Kevin any pain.

Well, not physical anyway.

What Leo does is take a very thorough sniff. A sniff loud enough for the neighborhood cats to overhear and take shelter.

"Wow," Bernard says. "The dog has got his whole head up in there."

"Do you think the photographer carries bacon in his butt?" Michael asks.

"Cluster together again," Kevin says to the four of us, acting as if nothing is happening.

We exchange glances and then do as Kevin says. I mean, Leo is happy to keep sniffing, and if Kevin wants a dog in his crotch, who are we to judge?

Oh, and needless to say, the smiles on the next bunch of photos are pretty genuine.

When the friends shoot is done, I take pity on Kevin and take Leo back to the soon-to-be-replaced handler.

"Okay," Kevin says with a solemness you would not expect from a guy who's just had his dignity sniffed away by a big, wet nose. "Now the newlyweds."

As soon as my friends stampede away, Jane floats over to my side, looking equal parts gorgeous and overwhelmed.

"I like to start the newlyweds shoot with the Gaze Pose," Kevin says. "It's the one where the couple look deeply into each other's eyes. It's a great warmup for what follows."

Complying, I meet Jane's eyes and instantly get lost in their amber depths. As if from a far distance, I hear Kevin say, "Got it. Perfect. Now let's do the next pose... The Kiss."

CHAPTER 31

Jane

Another kiss?

With Adrian?

I still haven't recovered from the one at the church—the best thing to ever happen to my lips... and the bits attached to them too.

That kiss was so universe shattering that I've had to keep reminding myself that this wedding is fake ever since. Which is why, if we kiss again, I don't think I—

Adrian's lips touch mine, and my ruminations are short circuited. All I feel is his tongue gently penetrating my mouth, his hand on my lower back, his warm breath—

"Turn her more to the right," a voice—Kevin's?—says, and even that doesn't seem to ruin the moment.

Adrian keeps kissing me as I feel myself being deliciously manhandled into a more photogenic position.

"Great," Kevin says. "Keep it up."

Adrian deepens the kiss, and I feel like I'm floating

out of my body—like my lips are the only physical part of me while the rest becomes as light as the ghost of a helium balloon.

Miss Miller—or rather Mrs. Westfield—finds this public display of affection gauche, even if performed with one's lawfully wedded husband. Unless, of course, this is the start of a bedding ceremony to add legitimacy to the marriage, in which case it should proceed posthaste.

"That's it," Kevin says.

Adrian doesn't stop, nor do I.

There are giggles in the room.

Kevin clears his throat a few times.

To my huge disappointment, Adrian gently pulls away.

Bringing my hand to my lips, I catch my breath.

My mom and grandma wink at me while my sister makes a gagging face. One of Adrian's friends tells us to save some for the wedding night.

Speaking of said friends, they are almost as hot as Adrian himself—and he's set the bar pretty high. Is this proof that the rich are secretly genetically engineering their offspring for good looks? It's a better conspiracy than the one about Elvis walking on the moon instead of Neil Armstrong.

"Get some air," Kevin says to Adrian. "I'm going to do some Jane-only poses."

And so he does, first by snapping some pictures of me pretending to write my vows, then ones where I slip on my shoes. Next, a giant bouquet is brought over, and

Kevin takes a picture of me staring at it like a hungry goat.

By the time I show off my veil and the train of my dress, I'm somewhat recovered from the kiss, and just in time because Kevin then announces that he wants us to do something called the V pose, and that it involves Adrian.

"Stand next to each other," Kevin orders. "Hips touching."

As soon as we comply, my breathing becomes heavier.

"Touch foreheads," Kevin says.

Did he just say touch—

Indeed. Adrian leans in, gazes warmly into my eyes, and grabs my hand.

Oh, my. Am I still a virgin? With all the feels in my panties, I'm not so sure anymore.

"Now let's do The Stack," Kevin says. "Jane, you stare into the distance—like you're seeing your future together. Adrian, stand behind her and wrap your arms around her. Then look at that same future."

My mom and grandma ooh and ahh while Adrian's friends say something snarky.

As his arms wrap around me, I melt on the spot like The Wicked Witch.

"Now take the veil," Kevin says. "And snuggle under it."

This is fake.

All fake.

"Kiss her shoulder, and we'll put a balcony behind you," Kevin says.

Fake, I tell myself.

Resting foreheads.

Fake.

Forehead kiss.

Fake.

Kiss from behind.

Fake or not, if Kevin doesn't stop this soon, the next pose will be called Jane Climbs Adrian Like a Tree.

CHAPTER 32

Adrian

What's this pose called? Downward Facing Doggie Style? Hard as a Mountain? Cock Tease Dolphin?

I have no idea, but there is a very real chance I'm going to end up with the worst case of blue balls ever recorded by a groom on his wedding day. Yet the torture-by-arousal continues for what feels like hours. Finally, when Yoda is about to explode, Kevin says that he has all the pictures he needs.

Perfect. Is there time for me to swing by the honeymoon suite and take an ice bath?

Nope. The wedding planner rushes in, panting, and informs us that we're late for our preparations for the grand entrance.

I grab Jane's hand as we're shepherded out of the room, and then we "prepare," which was a euphemism for hearing a boring lecture and waiting. Finally, the DJ announces that Mr. and Mrs. Westfield are about to walk together for the first time, and we enter to loud cheers and smiles all around.

As we're seated at our honorary spots—made to look like thrones, of course—I see Jane's jaw drop. Ah. She's noticed. It took some string pulling, but there they are—a few of the actors from the cast of *Bridgerton*, dressed in their outfits from the show.

Before Jane can recover, the DJ speaks up.

"And now, the newlyweds will have their first dance... the waltz."

Blushing, Jane beams at me.

I stand up and extend my hand to her. Soon, much to Yoda's discomfort, we begin to waltz.

"Did I mention this is like a fairytale wedding?" Jane whispers into my ear after a spin turn.

"Maybe once," I whisper back, and it takes all my willpower not to nibble on her dainty earlobe.

"Well, it is," she says. "When I get married for real, I'm not even going to bother with a ceremony because there's no way it will compare. I'll just head over to City Hall and call it a day."

I hate the idea of her getting married to someone who isn't me. What's wrong with me? Whatever it is, it's a major problem because on top of being jealous, I whisper, "The secret paparazzi are taking pictures. Would you mind another kiss for the cameras?"

What am I doing? I have no evidence that the paparazzi are actually taking pictures right now. It's almost as if I'm trying to—

Jane moistens her lips, blushes, and nods.

Fuck.

I lean in.

Jane rises on tiptoes.

The crowd goes silent.

We kiss. Just like the prior two times, it's transcendent. Better than any sex I've had.

My time perception goes out the window. I have no idea how long I kiss her, exploring every silky crevice of her mouth, tasting the softness of her lips, inhaling her sweet-scented breath. It's not until the waltz music stops and everyone claps thunderously that I snap out of the trance and rip myself away from Jane.

"Oh my," Jane gasps. "I need a drink."

"Great idea." I lead her back to our thrones, pop a champagne bottle, and pour us each a flute.

"And now," the DJ announces, "the best man will give a speech."

Best man? I wonder who has the balls to claim—

Of course.

Michael leaps to his feet.

I gulp down my flute, pour another, and repeat the process.

"I'd like to tell a story about how thoughtful Adrian is," Michael says.

Fuck. Not this story again. I down another glass of champagne and refill Jane's flute. Maybe if she's buzzed, she won't pay close attention to what's coming.

"Back in our school days, we visited his room a lot," Michael continues. "Which is how I found what I have since called The Notebook—though please don't confuse it with the vomit-inducing movie by the same name. In The Notebook, Adrian kept careful records of the things the girls he dated liked and disliked." He pulls out his phone. "I still have photos of the choiciest pages, and I'd like to share them with everyone, but especially Jane."

As Michael proceeds, Jane leans in and whispers, "Is any of it true?"

I nod ruefully. "It's the inventor in me, I guess. I always want the best way to get things done. The most efficient. The—"

Loud laughter drowns my next words.

Of course. Michael has got to the point in the journal where I wrote my careful ruminations on the subject of anal sex.

To my huge relief, Warren snatches the microphone away from Michael.

"This man is an impostor," Warren says. "I'm actually Adrian's best man, which is why I have an even better story to tell."

Fuck. What could he—

Ah. He tells them about the time he challenged me to invent something original (omitting the part about us being stoned), and how I answered the challenge by working out a process to make fabric from the casein in cheese.

Jane raises an eyebrow.

"It's true," I say. "In fact, I made a t-shirt from a particularly stinky cheese and gave it to Warren as a gift."

Jane laughs as Warren concludes the story with, "So

now, if evil cows from space devour all the cotton in the world, thanks to Adrian, we can still wear socks."

Before he can tell another anecdote, Bernard grabs the microphone, announces himself the *true* best man, and tells everyone that I was the inventor of the baby-mop onesie—a garment your toddler can wear as they crawl that cleans the floor at the same time.

"He plans to have Piper wear it." He gestures at where my daughter is sitting on Georgiana's lap. "But I say he'll end up spending more money on the bills for her therapy than he could ever save on a cleaning lady."

Jane furrows her brows.

"He made that up," I say. "But I did once attach regular mops to his tracksuit when he was so drunk that he was crawling."

She grins. "Drunk Idiot Mop Onesie™."

Before Bernard can start telling another story, someone cuts the sound to the microphone.

Fucking finally.

"Let us all thank the best men," the DJ says, imbuing the words with elephant-heavy sarcasm. "Now, please, go dance before it's time to enjoy your favorite wedding breakfast dishes."

Jane sighs. "Wedding breakfast is what they called the reception back in Victorian times."

Hmm. If wedding breakfast isn't literally a breakfast, Jane might mind some of the surprise dishes I've added to the main course, such as Eggs Benedict and French Toast.

The music starts playing, and it's a club-like remix of the theme from *Bridgerton*.

"Want to dance?" Jane shyly asks.

Refuse this offer I cannot, which means suffer Yoda will.

Downing my champagne, I get on my feet and extend a hand to Jane. "My lady."

She takes my hand. "Now that we're married, we're allowed to be less formal. Especially in private."

"Great," I say as I lead her to the middle of the dance floor. "I can finally call you Jelly Bean. Or would you prefer Janilla? Maybe J-Bone?"

"In that case, your nom de plume shall be Applesauce," she says. "Or Rio. Or Adieu. Or Audrey. Or just Drey. Maybe even Dr. Drey?"

I twirl her. "You win. You'll just be my Jane."

"I like that." Her cheeks turn pink. "And you'll be my Adrian."

Seriously, Yoda? *That* gets you going too?

As soon as the remix stops, a song by Céline Dion comes on, so we slow dance to that. Because I don't have any excuse to kiss Jane at this point, I fight the weird urge to do so.

"Hungry?" I ask Jane a couple of songs later.

She bites one of her delectable lips. "Ravenous."

Returning to the table, we sample the menu and find it all delicious.

Jane's family comes over, with Piper still sitting on Georgiana's hip and the bodyguard/nanny on their tail.

I kiss her cherubic cheek. Piper's, that is.

"Can the little one spend the night with me?" Georgiana asks.

I nod. "So long as you're willing to sleep in her nursery."

Jane's grandmother frowns. "At your place?"

"Correct."

"Isn't that where the wedding night is to take place?" Jane's grandmother asks, her frown deepening.

"We have a honeymoon suite," Jane says proudly. "In this hotel."

"The honeymoon suite." Jane's grandmother gives me a disturbingly lascivious wink. "I hope it has a swing."

She means a sex swing, right? Jane must think so too, because her cheeks deepen in color.

"A swing?" Mary asks curiously. "Why would the suite have—"

"I think that's our cue to leave," Georgiana says sternly, then leads her mother away, none too gently.

"But seriously," Mary demands. "What's the swing for?"

Jane gulps down a champagne flute. "I'll explain when you're much, much older."

"Eww, don't," Mary says. "I don't want swings ruined for me, ever."

As my little sister-in-law departs, the DJ announces that the cake is ready to be cut, so Jane and I head over to do the honors.

As per the tradition, I wrap my hand over Jane's—and, not surprisingly, I want to forego eating the cake and eat something that promises to be even more sweet.

Jane's pussy, in case that wasn't clear.

But I can't. For reasons. Good ones—even if I can't exactly recall what they are.

With the cake officially cut, I lead Jane back to the table, and we all attack the dessert.

I'm almost done with my cake when Jane's family comes back with Piper and her bodyguard.

"This was so much fun," Georgiana says. "But it's getting late, and the little one has been fussing."

"She has?" I walk up to Piper and kiss her forehead. Though there's a baby grin on her face now, I know she could fuss again at any moment, so I bid Georgiana and everyone a hearty goodbye. As soon as they leave, my fellow musketeers stop by and inform us that they're heading out too.

"Your bedtime already?" I can't help but snark at them.

"Burlesque show," Warren says. "Unless you're about to put one on here?"

I roll my eyes.

"Why do you care anyway?" Bernard asks me. "All you should be thinking of is the consummation of this marriage."

Jane turns beet red.

"Unless you already did it," Michael chimes in. "After the picture taking?"

Did I say beet? Make that red wine.

"Have fun at the alleged Burlesque show," I tell them

and switch my attention to the next person who is about to say goodbye.

Very soon, the party is over, with the likely journalist spies as the only people remaining.

Well, then, here's something for them to write about.

Standing up, I shout, "Okay, everyone! We're headed to the honeymoon suite."

With that, I pick up Jane in a bridal carry, and as people clap, I triumphantly stride out of the room.

CHAPTER 33

Jane

"Put me on the bed," I say breathlessly as Adrian carries me into the obscenely luxurious honeymoon suite. "I don't trust myself to stand."

Yep. My knees are wobbly, and not just because of the buzz from the champagne. I'm overdosing on dopamine and oxytocin, and it's all Adrian's fault. It was bad enough when he'd touch me, or dance with me, or smile at me, but being carried like this, pressed against his rock-hard chest and enveloped in his strong arms while breathing in his deliciously masculine scent, makes me swoony in a very real way.

The bed must be of the Alaskan King variety—a nine-foot square that could comfortably accommodate a dozen of the tallest NBA players... even if they were to have an orgy with their tallest counterparts from the WNBA.

Very gently, Adrian sets me down at the edge of the bed, right onto a thousand roses' worth of petals.

Yes, petals—and they're not the only honeymoon accoutrements scattered around the room. There are enough candles to create a major fire hazard, enough chocolates to give even the healthiest person diabetes, and enough heart-shaped balloons to lift an obese elephant.

It's all uber romantic and beyond my wildest GD wet dreams.

To put it another way, it's the universe taunting me with the fact that I'll stay a virgin tonight.

Gulping in a breath, I detect the smell of incense—and that combines with the aroma of the flowers to spin my head even faster.

Adrian starts to straighten, but our eyes lock.

Uh-oh.

Must look away.

Can't.

By Jove, I seriously can't tear my eyes away from him.

My infatuation must be obvious, but he's not looking away either. In fact, his gaze is rapt, and a muscle in his jaw twitches—begging me to lick it. And then nibble on that sharp cheekbone before I—

Mrs. Westfield firmly believes that one ought not to take certain liberties, even with one's husband.

Overcome by an irresistible impulse, I clutch his tie like a chlamydia-free koala grabbing a hold of a eucalyptus tree. My brain gives my arm a brazen command to pull Adrian down, but before the arm can execute said command, Adrian makes his move—probably because otherwise, he'd lose his license as a rake.

His mouth swoops in like a bird of prey, and his hands land near the bodice of my dress.

Yes!

All thoughts flee my head, and I lose myself in the kiss, aware only of the sweetness of the wedding cake on his breath and something very masculine that is purely Adrian.

The sound of silk and lace ripping thunders through the room.

He ripped my bodice!

Like in the best romance novels.

Holy smokes. Could it be? Am I finally going to get my GD?

It sure seems like it.

Adrian deepens the kiss, his tongue penetrating my mouth, giving me a prelude of the marital act as his hands slide down to my destroyed bodice, freeing my breasts and making my nipples tingle at the rush of cool air.

Please, for the love of all that is sacred about the institution of marriage, let him continue. If he stops, I shall go mad.

He doesn't stop. He kisses my neck, then slides down, capturing my hard-as-a-diamond nipple in his luxurious mouth.

A moan escapes my lips.

Growling low in his throat, Adrian yanks the ruined dress from my body in several impatient tugs before lifting his head to stare down at me.

I gulp, feeling deliciously exposed under his ravenous

gaze. The fact that he's completely dressed only intensifies the sensation. My skin turns hot as a blush covers my entire body.

"You're gorgeous," Adrian whispers hoarsely—or I think he does because he then drags his tongue down my belly, jumbling the last remnants of my brain.

Dazedly, I wonder where that tongue is headed. And then I know. It's what my books would call "my most secret place."

Is he about to—

He is. Giving my clit the most sensual of licks, Adrian proceeds with his tender ministrations, each one eliciting a moan from my mouth.

A tsunami builds in my core.

Panting, I grasp his hair, pulling him closer to my sex. "Yes, yes!" The tension gathering inside me is so strong, so overwhelming, that only seconds pass before the tsunami makes landfall.

With a cry, I come, my toes curling as hot ecstasy rushes down my spine.

Panting, I open my heavy eyelids.

Huh. Did I pass out for a second there?

Last I checked, Adrian was dressed, but now, he's deliciously naked—and his manhood is bigger and harder than in any of my fantasies, so much so there's a not-unpleasant quiver in the center of my womanhood.

And yes, the "hoods" mean cock and pussy, respectively.

"That was amazing," I breathe out.

His lips quirk with masculine pride. "I'm glad."

I reach for his cock, but as my fingers brush the velvety skin, Adrian draws away.

"I want to return the favor," I explain shyly.

His eyes gleam, and his voice is husky. "As much as I'd love that, I want to be inside you."

Gulp. How can this one sentence make me go from sexually satiated to its complete opposite?

"Assuming," he continues, "that the honor of GDing you is still on the table. I would understand if—"

"Yes," I gasp. "You can have me on the table."

He smiles roguishly. "For your first time, how about we use a bed?"

I nod with way too much enthusiasm.

"You know it might hurt, right?" Adrian asks. "I'll do my best to be gentle, but—"

"Yes. I'm ready." I dart a worried glance at his beautiful-and-hopefully-not-too-big deflowering instrument.

That which I'm looking at twitches... and maybe winks at me.

"And you know what to expect in general?" Adrian continues softly.

"I've seen lots of porn," I say with a confidence I do not feel.

Hey, my preparation is better than that of any of the heroines from historical romances, where they either get a clue from farm animals or awkward chats with their mothers and other married ladies. Case in point, Daphne from *Bridgerton* didn't even know about the pull-out method, or sperm in general. Just one cum shot would've educated her, not to mention a bukkake video, where the actresses borderline drown in the stuff.

"Real life can be different from porn," Adrian says, his eyes crinkling in amusement. "But either way, do you have any requests or suggestions?"

"No choking, please," I say earnestly. "And maybe don't slap my face with your dick... this time around. Oh, and if your attitude toward anal has changed since you wrote in your journal, let's skip that for today too, at least as far as my butt goes."

He nods solemnly, even as the crinkles around his eyes deepen. "You got it." His gaze turns more serious. "You should also know that I'm clean."

Shit. I should've asked that first and foremost. "I'm also clean," I blurt. "And you already know about my IUD."

Adrian's reply is to kiss my neck again. Then his fingers feather through my hair, ruining my coiffure. I inhale sharply as his cock presses against my belly, and I feel heat pooling just a few inches below it.

His mouth retraces the path from earlier, down my belly and over to my clit.

Wait a second. I thought—

He laps between my folds once again, and thought becomes the furthest thing from my mind. Reveling in the pleasure coiling inside me, I writhe underneath him, growing desperate for the release.

His clever tongue keeps going.

My hands ball into the sheets. Here we go. Another record-breaking orgasm is about to—

But no. Adrian pulls away just as I am on the brink. The head of his cock is now where his tongue was a second ago, teasing my entrance and driving me insane in equal measure.

Before I can let out a cry of frustration, Adrian captures my lips in a scorching kiss.

The heat inside me intensifies. I wouldn't have guessed that tasting myself would be such a turn on, but here we are—and now I need him inside me so badly I may scream.

As if sensing my desperation, Adrian gently enters me, and there's a moment when pleasure is tinged with pain, but the pleasure quickly wins out—likely due to all the endorphins having their way with my opiate receptors. All I want is to reach that elusive orgasm that I was teased with, and lo and behold, it starts building anew, faster than I thought possible.

"That's it," Adrian grunts as he thrusts deeper. "Come with me. Now."

What choice do I have? My inner muscles quiver around his cock, and I dig my nails into his back as I come on the next thrust.

Adrian groans in pleasure and grinds into me. I must've squeezed him just right because I feel the warm wetness of his release as another aftershock of pleasure bursts forth inside me.

Wow. That was... wow.

I can neither move nor open my eyes.

I bet there's a blissed-out expression on my no-longer-virginal face.

I hear Adrian move off the bed.

Whatever.

He comes back, and a warm, wet cloth presses against my center.

Yeah. This is bliss. And it continues as Adrian wraps his body around mine.

It might be my sleepy brain, but I can almost visualize our fake marriage transforming into something. Something real. Something where I can feel this way every day.

If I could, I'd bottle this moment forever, but alas, I drift off to sleep.

CHAPTER 34

Adrian

As Jane falls asleep in my arms, the enormity of what has just happened hits me like a shot from the triple barrel cannon that DaVinci invented but never built.

I slept with Jane. Devirginized her, to be precise. If this were the time period she likes to read about, the honorable thing for me to do would be to marry her— except that has already happened.

Fuck. It was the best sex of my life. And that's not a hyperbole—it was genuinely the best. The scorching chemistry that simmered between us all this time was, if anything, an under-promise. The real sex was so much better than anything my mind conjured up during my lonely dates with my fist. And I had to hold back due to her virginity. I can't even imagine how good it'll be between us once—

No. We can't. We shouldn't. Her GD, as Jane called it, shouldn't have happened, but since it has, the only thing I can control is what happens next—which should be nothing. The hearing requires all my focus, and Jane is too delicious of a distraction. Worse yet, a single wrong move on my end could jeopardize the very reason for our fake marriage.

My chest feels peculiarly tight as I gently extricate myself from Jane's soft, small body, grab a robe, and quietly go out onto the giant balcony.

The fresh air doesn't help. I still feel an unsettling combination of guilt, regret, and, worst of all, burning desire.

I want more Jane. I want it so badly I can taste it. But I can't do this to Piper. I can't risk losing her.

Speaking of Piper... I pull out my phone, and some of the tension drains from my shoulders as I pull up the baby monitor app and see her. She's sleeping like the baby that she is.

This, right here, is why I must pump the brakes on whatever it is that's happening between Jane and me.

With a sigh, I open the email from Bob with the documents I need to review for the hearing. A very long hour later, I'm glad life's circumstances didn't force me into a career in the justice system, but I'm grateful for those who are willing to do this kind of work.

I also still ache to hold Jane.

I contemplate sneaking out to another room to avoid the temptation, but I decide that wouldn't be fair to Jane. I don't want her to feel like this was a one-night stand.

Quietly, I return to bed and stretch out as far away

from her as the giant bed allows. All I want is to close the distance between us, but that wouldn't be wise.

I need to sleep. More importantly, I need to let her sleep.

We'll discuss everything in the morning.

CHAPTER 35

Jane

My first thought as I wake up is to question whether the events of last night were real because it was all too much like a dream.

I peek through my eyelashes.

I'm in the giant bed, in the honeymoon suite, with Adrian on the other side of the bed. And I'm sore in—

Mrs. Westfield would advise against naming such delicate places even within a lady's private thoughts.

All this means that if my GD was a dream, it's continuing.

"You awake?" Adrian whispers, scooting closer.

I turn his way. "Hopefully."

He tucks a strand of my hair behind my ear. "How do you feel?"

I bite my lip. "Disappointingly, the same as usual."

He arches an eyebrow. "Disappointingly?"

I mock sigh. "I always thought I'd feel different after losing my virginity."

He cocks his head. "Different how?"

"Older. More mature. Wiser."

"Ah. And you don't?"

"I'm thinking we may need to repeat what we did last night a few dozen more times before all those things kick in."

His good humor evaporates, and he looks distinctly uncomfortable. "Jane... I'm not sure that's a good idea."

His words hit me like an ice bucket challenge, proving beyond a shadow of doubt that this is stark reality, not the fantasy land of my GD dreams.

"Us sleeping together isn't a good idea?" I hear myself demand, though I'm not sure why I'm punishing myself this way.

He draws back. "I'm sorry. I had hoped we'd talk about this later. Calmly."

Calmly? There's no way on this earth I can think about this calmly. Not after I stupidly started to believe that last night meant something. That I could have hope for the two of us.

My stomach turns into a stone, and a wave of nausea rolls over me.

How could I be so naïve? So very virginal? I should've remembered that having sex is like a good sneeze for a rake like him. But even then, why would he deny me something so meaningless to him as a sneeze?

Then it hits me, and I'm glad I'm on the bed because my legs feel too weak to support my weight.

"You think last night was a mistake?" I half state, half

ask. He must. That's what this is about. He's a hot billionaire playboy, and I'm a plain Jane who was probably a boring lay on top of that. Having sex with me for him was probably like having one of those half-sneezes you sometimes get when your nose is itchy—completely unsatisfying.

In fact, it's a marvel he stooped to having sex with me in the first place. It was probably due to his self-enforced celibacy, combined with his rakish nature and the romantic atmosphere of the wedding.

Or maybe he was more calculating in bedding me. Maybe he's going to make it so the bloody sheets end up in the hands of some paparazzo, ensuring that the world knows our marriage was consummated, à la medieval times. That would be worth an unpleasant sneeze. Or maybe he was concerned they'd check my hymen at the hearing to make sure our marriage wasn't a sham. Or—

He gently props up my chin with his fingers. "Last night was not a mistake, but if we keep being intimate, we'll find ourselves in a real relationship, and those often end. If that were to happen, where would it leave Piper's hearing?"

Another ice-cold bucket right in the face. Now on top of rejected, I also feel like a selfish brat. That little girl deserves to have a father as awesome as Adrian in her life, while all I'm worried about is my fragile ego and overactive libido.

But still. If he felt this way, he shouldn't have GD'd me in the first place. It's unfair. He treats his dog better than this—he told me so himself. Something about not being able to miss sex if you've never had it.

"You're right," I say. "We shouldn't do that again." I wish I could add that it's because I wouldn't want to anyway, but I'm not that good of a liar.

Is that a glimmer of regret in his eyes? No. That's just wishful thinking on my part.

Suddenly, I feel much too naked, so I drag the blanket all the way to my chin and say, "Can you give me some privacy?"

With a sigh, he gets off the bed, giving me an unadulterated view of his out-of-this-world body. Then he grabs a robe and hides it all, which feels like a crime against nature.

"Here." He tosses another robe my way, then turns his back to me.

Must not sniffle. That would be worse than being naked in front of him again.

I put on the robe and struggle to get my turbulent emotions under control.

Acting as if he didn't just shatter my world, Adrian proceeds to order in a gourmet room service breakfast. I go into the shower, and when I re-emerge, the food is already here. It's pretty and smells great, but it tastes like straw laced with sewage—possibly because of the knot of tears stuck in my throat. The conversation during the meal is pretty much nonexistent, due to that same knot. I'm not sure what his problem is, but whatever. I'm going to treat our relationship, such as it is, as purely a work arrangement, so there's no need for us to banter.

Who knew that my awkward interactions with Mrs. Corsica would come in handy? As soon as the breakfast is over, I ask Adrian when we're headed home.

"Whenever you wish," he says.

I press my lips together. "How about we go now?"

Even though we're officially married, Adrian doesn't carry me over the threshold when we arrive home. Instead, we go our separate ways and don't have lunch or dinner together—all my choice, and I stand by it.

That night, I cry myself to sleep. The next day, when we come across each other, we again talk about the weather. It's the most civil interaction I can manage, and even that is taxing. I continue to avoid him as much as living in the same penthouse allows, and several days pass in the same tense yet civil manner.

Then, on Thursday, Adrian walks in while I'm reading in his library and tells me that *Queen Charlotte* has come out on Netflix, and that we should watch it together.

"No, thank you," I say firmly.

He thinks we can be friends again? Fat fucking chance!

He cocks his head. "It's a *Bridgerton* spin-off. I thought that was your favorite series."

"I want to read the book first. They haven't released it just yet."

I'm actually dying to watch the show, but I plan to

tell him I hated the book and that I'm skipping the show... and then I'll watch it either stealthily by myself or after our arrangement is over.

He grimaces and takes a step toward me. "Look, Jane... I don't want us to keep acting like strangers."

"You don't?" I ask bitterly. "But isn't that safer? If we talk about anything of substance, we might have a quarrel, and if that gets bad enough, it could jeopardize the hearing."

Petty, I know, but the logic is identical to his.

"Fair enough," he says with a sigh and leaves.

The days following that conversation are as opposite of honeymoon bliss as it gets. We don't even talk about the weather anymore, just the hearing, which is quickly approaching.

The only bright spots in the dull monotony of my days are when Piper visits, but even those are tinged with heartache because by now, I'm in love with the little girl, and I know I won't see her once Adrian has no more use for me.

Oh, and did I mention seeing him be a good daddy is the most potent aphrodisiac?

It is, and it doesn't help matters.

The minutes stretch into hours and days, and finally, it's the night before the hearing. I expect it to be as uneventful as all the nights preceding it, but a distant shout wakes me up around three a.m.

What the hell? Is Leo up to his sheep shenanigans?

Overcome by the same curiosity that usually gets

women in horror flicks killed, I put on a robe and open my door to peek into the hallway.

And wish I hadn't.

It's Sydney.

As in, Adrian's baby mama. As in, the last person I expected to see outside of tomorrow's hearing.

Her boob is out as she's struggling to pull on her dress, and her hair is a mess.

Even though my brain hasn't made the conscious leap just yet, my veins fill with liquid nitrogen.

It only gets worse.

A fully naked Adrian comes running down the hallway. Spotting me, he freezes in place. His voice is choked. "Jane... this isn't what it looks like."

Before he can say anything else, I slam my door closed.

My heart is hammering in my chest, and I'm holding in a scream—one that would probably shatter glass if I let it loose.

There's a knock, followed by Adrian's tight voice. "We need to talk."

"I don't want to talk," I somehow manage to say.

"Please," he says. "I wanted—"

Using all my willpower, I say evenly, "The hearing is tomorrow. I need some sleep." Like I could sleep after what I just saw.

There's a beat of silence. "You're right," he finally says. "But we have to talk after."

Sure we do. He's probably just relieved that I'm still going to the hearing.

Which I am—for Piper, not for him. I'll go even though all I want is to be done with this charade so I can go home to Staten Island, eat Mom's chicken soup, and cry for a week.

Pointlessly, I get back into bed, my thoughts buzzing in my head like agitated wasps.

This isn't what it looks like.

It looks like they had sex, and things got wild. What else could they be doing naked together at night?

I squeeze my eyes shut, but that only worsens the images flashing through my mind. Images inspired by all the porn I've watched, except featuring Adrian and his ex instead of big-dicked actors. Not that his is small.

Wait, what am I even thinking about?

Ugh, I need to stop this pointless rumination. He doesn't owe me anything. Ours isn't a real relationship, despite my GD, which, as we've already established, was the equivalent of an unsatisfying sneeze.

In my face.

But it hurts. It feels like a betrayal—much more so than his words the morning after our wedding. At least then he'd claimed to act in the best interests of Piper. Unless... Did he sleep with Sydney to reassure himself that the hearing is still necessary? Like, if the sex went well, maybe they could make it work?

No, that doesn't make a lot of sense.

Perhaps he did it as a hedge? If so, that might even be clever, in a psychopathic sort of way. Remind Sydney of the heaven that is his cock, and then if the hearing doesn't go his way, he can just invite her back, and she would come—she's only human.

Fucking hell.

My throat tightens with the same scream I've been holding back.

Is it possible that they have been sleeping together this whole time? Is that the real reason why he didn't want to do it with me?

I know—and hate the idea that—they've done it at least once, since Piper is proof of that.

But why bother with the hearing if they have an ongoing sex life? Could it be that they have some kind of weird/unhealthy sex? A hate-fucking addiction or something? Is that what the shouting was about?

Or worse, is it possible he just likes her for sex but hates her company?

It could be. He has the exact opposite setup with me. Or at least it seemed like he enjoyed my company back when we were on speaking terms.

Maybe between the two of us, he's found the perfect partner?

The thought constricts my lungs, making it difficult to breathe.

I know one thing for sure at this point.

Going to sleep is just a distant fantasy.

"We'll talk after the hearing," Adrian says when I meet him by the elevator.

"Sure." I rub my bloodshot eyes. "Whatever you say."

I don't clarify if he's talking about his wild sex with Sydney or something else. Either way, I'm still in no state to have anything approximating a "talk."

We enter the elevator, and as soon as he presses the button for the lobby, he starts reading some sort of printout—no doubt related to the hearing.

The whole ride in the limo, he continues to read the same papers, and I try prepping too, as best as I can.

When we enter the courtroom, I quickly spot my mom, who's here to provide moral support for Adrian, though I wonder if she would've come if I'd told her about the post-GD cold war and about last night. Taking a seat next to her, I ignore Adrian when he takes his seat and listen to the proceedings.

To my left, Mom stares at Tristan, Sydney's father. Before I can tell her that this man is off limits and why, she looks at Juliet—Sydney's mother—and then at Sydney herself. The whole time, Mom's expression is extremely strange.

I wonder about it for a moment, but I don't have time to dwell on it because looking at Sydney resurrects all the feelings from last night. I grit my teeth until my jaw hurts and ball my hands into tight fists on my lap.

Meanwhile, the lawyers do their thing, starting with Adrian's side. They make a case for him being a good father and an upstanding citizen who has renounced his rakish ways. The judge is hard to read, but I think she's buying it. When the other side starts to speak, Sydney darts a nasty glance our way, and something about it turns my insides all clammy.

She's too confident. Almost like she's already gloating. But why—

"Please have a look at the screen," one of Sydney's lawyers says at that exact moment.

We all do, but I'm probably the first to realize what it is that I'm seeing—and my whole body goes rigid as I do.

Up on the screen is the secret contract that I signed. The very same one that outlines the fact that my marriage with Adrian is fake—which is exactly what the lawyer points out next.

People turn my way with knowing expressions. "Ah, that explains it," their faces seem to be saying. "That's why a guy like him would marry a woman like you. As a farce."

My face burns, and I sneak a peek at Adrian. He's staring at me with an extremely betrayed expression. He clearly thinks I gave Sydney the document, even though I did nothing of the sort.

My mind races, looking for the answers. Only one comes to mind: Sydney's people must've hacked into the app account I set up and got a hold of the document. Not that Adrian will believe that.

And I guess it ultimately doesn't matter because this is it. I fucked up. Adrian will not get custody of Piper, and it's my fault.

I feel the strongest urge to run, but instead, as if turning into a zombie, I shakily get to my feet and stumble out of the courtroom.

I know it's cowardly, but I don't want to see the expression on Adrian's face when he realizes how bad this really is. Nor do I want him to tell me he never wants to see me again.

That bit is obvious.

In the corner of my eye, I see my mom—and for some reason, Tristan—leap to their feet and rush after me.

What the hell? Maybe Sydney's father just needs the bathroom?

But no.

As I exit onto the street, I see Mom grabbing Tristan's elbow as he yells for me to stop.

They fiercely argue about something so I sprint over to them, ready to defend Mom from whatever the dude's problem is.

When I'm within hearing distance, they go silent and look guilty.

Seriously? What fresh hell is this? With everything that has happened, the last thing I need is a weird mystery.

"What's going on?" I demand.

Tristan examines my face like he's never seen faces until today. "Are you... Georgiana's daughter?"

"Umm, yes."

He peers at me even more intently. "And you're twenty-three years and-four-months old?"

And four months? What, are we back in kindergarten?

"Don't," Mom says to him. "Let us talk first."

"Don't what?" I demand. "Is there something going on between you two?"

That's the most logical solution, but—

"I'm sorry," Tristan says to Mom. Then he turns to me. "I'm your father."

CHAPTER 36
Jane

I stand there, speechless and fighting the urge to simply run away because there's a limit to what a woman can handle in such a short amount of time, and I was past said limit long before this bombshell.

Could he be lying?

I dart a glance at my mom. She's pale and not even denying it. Which means it's the truth.

This stranger is my father.

But is he really?

Gritting my teeth, I examine Tristan's face the same way he's been doing to me all this time.

Hell's bells. We have features in common, so it could actually be true. But...

"How?" I ask, not sure whom. I'm feeling an odd numbness at this point, like someone else is speaking for me.

"It was as I told you. We met at a nightclub," Mom says.

"And it was just that once," Tristan says, sounding a bit defensive.

"The number of times wouldn't have made you any less married," Mom says to him. Turning to me, she adds, "And he had his own baby on the way as well."

His own baby. I clutch my chest as my overwhelmed brain finally makes the connection.

Tristan is Sydney's father too—so she is the baby he had on the way. If this is all true, this makes Sydney my half-sister. And we do share amber eyes, black hair, and small faces—I noticed that when I met her, but I didn't realize the significance, of course.

How Jerry Springer. A guy has come between me and my half-sister. So much for sisters before misters.

Then another thing hits me. This makes Piper my half-niece.

I like this realization. A lot. It even explains a few things, like why she felt like my flesh and blood the moment I met her. Because she is. We share twelve-and-a-half percent of our DNA.

Then again, she's such a sweetie I would've loved her regardless.

"—swear I didn't know she was underage," I hear Tristan say, and that tidbit drags me back to the conversation. "She told me she was eighteen."

"All women lie about their age," Mom says defensively. "And you could've checked."

He nods. "I could've done a lot of things differently back then."

"You can say that again," Mom snaps. She turns to

me. "When I told him I was pregnant, he gave me money —for silence and an abortion."

"Hold on." I struggle to catch my breath. "You always said you never saw my father after the one-night stand. That you didn't know his name." Tristan winces at this last one, but I continue. "You couldn't have known you were pregnant the morning after the one-night stand."

Mom glares at Tristan. "This is why I wanted to talk to her first." Turning to me, she says, "I'm sorry I lied. Between him being married and pushing the abortion, I thought you'd be better off without him."

Tristan looks at me earnestly. "I didn't push, I merely suggested it as an option, and I'm very sorry about that. With Georgiana being a minor, I was afraid I'd end up in jail—and as we've already discussed, I had a baby on the way."

I rub my throbbing temples. "So... until today, you thought I didn't exist?"

Not that this would make me forgive him, but—

He grimaces. "I felt guilty about the way I acted toward your mother, so I tracked her down a couple of years later to apologize."

"More like to make sure I'd keep quiet," Mom mutters.

"Which is when I learned that she decided to keep you," Tristan continues. "So I offered to help in any way I could, but she told me she didn't want me in your life— and I decided to respect her wishes."

"More like he decided to let sleeping dogs lie," Mom corrects.

Tristan sighs. "Maybe that's true, but as time went on, I regretted it, more and more with every passing year."

I shake off the daze gripping me. "Clearly not enough to find me or speak with me." I point toward the courtroom. "If you want to know how a father *should* act, just look at the lengths Adrian is going to in order to be in his daughter's life."

Tristan takes a step back. "I wasn't sure what I'd even say if I approached you."

"How about, 'Hi, I'm the sperm donor,'" I grit out.

Tristan slowly blinks. "I guess I deserve that moniker. And you're right. It doesn't matter what I would've said. Just reaching out was important, and I blew it. I was a coward, and I'm sorry for that too. But when I saw you today—and realized that I've already met you—I couldn't hold it in anymore."

My chest tightens. "And here we are."

Mom catches my gaze. "I'm sorry I didn't tell you the whole truth about him. Please don't hate me. I thought what I did was for the best."

"I'd never hate you," I say, even though at this moment I am pretty mad at her. Grudgingly, I admit, "I'm not sure how I would've acted in your shoes."

"Moot point," Mom says proudly. "You did not get pregnant as a teen."

"I hope you don't hate me either," Tristan says. "And

that you'd consider getting to know me... in any way you're comfortable with."

Has someone cranked up the heat outside? "I'll have to think about it," I manage to say.

"Thank you," he says so earnestly I feel a pang of something he doesn't deserve.

"On one condition," I add, surprising even myself.

"Name it," he says.

"Make it so that I get to be in Piper's life, regardless of how things go in there." I gesture at the courtroom.

If I get to see Piper again, my heart would hurt a little bit less.

Tristan only hesitates for a heartbeat before he says, "I'll do everything in my power to make that happen. But it would have to be only you. If things don't go Adrian's way, I don't think Sydney would let him—"

I gasp as a terrible realization occurs to me. "Once Adrian learns Sydney and I are related, he'll think I helped her—especially if I get to see Piper and he can't."

"I doubt he'll think that," Mom says.

She thinks too highly of her fake son-in-law.

I turn to Tristan. "Do you know how Sydney got that stupid document?"

He hesitates longer this time. "Even if I tell you, and you run back in there and tell them, it won't change the outcome," he finally says.

"Obviously," I say. "The djinni is out now."

He shifts from foot to foot. "The help came from a disgruntled security guard who used to work in Adrian's building. The guard claims she helped because she and her husband had to start over at a new workplace because of you, but I think she was money hungry and rationalizing. In any case, she gave Sydney the password you set to access the building and suggested that you're not careful with passwords in general. The hope was that you'd used the same password with the app Adrian likes to use for all his legal documents—and that turned out to be the case."

Oh. Damn. It was Susan. She even chastised me for using recognizable words in said password—but I didn't change my ways at all and went ahead and used the exact same password for that stupid app. I also completely forgot that Susan had to get a new job because I made a big deal about seeing a naked statue of her in Adrian's gallery.

"Please bear in mind this all happened before I knew who you were," Tristan says. "And that Sydney is just trying to do what she thinks is best for her child."

Is he comparing my mom's actions to those of Sydney? No, that would mean he disapproves of his own daughter. Unless—

"This is all too much," I say, mostly to myself.

"Here." Tristan hands me his business card, and it takes me what feels like ten minutes to decide if I should stick it in one of my pockets or in my purse—that's how overwhelmed I am at this point.

"Can we talk?" Mom says.

I shake my head. "I need to be alone." And not just because of the man standing next to us. The one back in the courtroom is a far bigger culprit.

Mom grimaces. "I understand. I'm here if you need me."

I swallow, my eyes burning, and run for the nearest yellow cab.

When the cabbie asks where to go, I tell him to take me home.

"And where is home?" he asks, his voice a mixture of kindness and exasperation.

"Just take me to the Staten Island Ferry," I say.

After I take the ferry, I'll take a bus since I don't have millions in my bank account yet, and now I probably never will.

But I don't care about the money. I'd give it all to undo this clusterfuck of a day. And here is what bothers me the most about this whole thing.

The person I desperately want to discuss all this with is Adrian.

CHAPTER 37

Adrian

I watch Jane leave the courtroom and realize I fucked up. For a moment, I considered that she might've betrayed me, and she read that on my face.

After that moment passed, I knew she couldn't have done it, no matter how mad she was about my earlier actions. Alas, now it's too late. I should run after her, but I can't. Piper needs me here, at the hearing.

In fact, I've already missed something Bob was saying, though I think the gist of it was, "That kind of information could only be obtained by illegal hacking, which doesn't speak well for Sydney's character."

"That doesn't make his marriage real," someone counters—though their actual words have more legalese.

I leap to my feet, propelled by an uncontrollable impulse. "It doesn't matter how my relationship with Jane started. As we got to know each other, I genuinely fell in love with her, and now I plan to keep her as my wife forever."

As the words leave my mouth, I realize that it's the truth.

The reason her silent treatment hurts so much is because I love Jane and I hate how unhappy she seems.

Well, no more. I'm going to find a way to fix things between us.

Out of the corner of my eye, I notice Sydney going pale. I guess she believes my declaration, and it must rid her of all the last-ditch fantasies she's been harboring, the ones where the two of us magically end up together despite everything.

"If my marriage is the deciding factor for custody," I continue, "I'm willing to sign a document that stating that if Jane and I were ever to get divorced, Sydney would—"

"My client is just joking," Bob interjects.

It's a good thing he stopped me. What if Jane—

"It doesn't matter anyway," the judge says. She faces Sydney's side. "Is there more?"

They tell her there isn't.

"In that case, I'm going to make the ruling," she says.

Heart hammering in my throat, I listen so intently I can hear someone's stomach rumble in the first row. Then, as the judge speaks, a feeling of weightlessness overcomes my body, not unlike how I feel when inside a sensory deprivation chamber. I'm also so happy about what I hear that I want to dance a jig because, when stripped of all the legalese, the ruling is exactly what I've worked so hard to accomplish—fifty/fifty custody.

As in, I can be fully present in Piper's life.

A wide grin spreads over my face, and I almost hug Bob, but then I downgrade the gesture to a handshake. I've never been so elated. An actual warmth radiates through my body.

I turn to kiss Jane in my excitement, only to remember that she left.

Fuck.

The happiness dims.

How could I have forgotten? Jane left, and she's even more upset with me than before.

"Am I needed here?" I ask Bob.

"No. That was it. Congratulations, sir. We can hash everything out with the other side without you pres—"

Not waiting for the rest of it, I sprint out of the courtroom—where I bump into Georgiana, who is talking with Tristan, of all people.

Very odd.

"Have you seen Jane?" I ask her.

"She took a yellow cab," Tristan answers.

If I had more time, I'd ask why he's keeping track of Jane's movements, but as is, I just look at Jane's mom for confirmation.

She nods.

"Where did she go?" I ask.

"Home." Georgiana waves her phone. "She texted me. She's about halfway to the Staten Island Ferry."

I take out my own phone and text my limo driver to

come get me, adding 911 at the end to highlight the highest of urgencies.

"Your best bet is to catch her at the Ferry terminal," Georgiana continues. "The next one departs at one thirty."

I check my watch and frown. We can just barely make it if we break every speed limit.

Tires screeching, the limo pulls up to the curb.

I leap inside and promise the driver a six-digit bonus if we get to our destination on time. Maybe that was too much because the limo torpedoes forward, and we fly through the busy Manhattan streets as if filming *The Fast and the Furious*.

I call Jane.

She doesn't pick up.

I text her.

Same result.

Before I know it, we screech to a stop at the White-hall Terminal, and I run out of the limo and up the escalator, skipping stairs as I go.

Fuck. Jane is nowhere in sight, and the time is 1:32, which means the ferry is already loading.

I take my phone out and desperately call Jane one more time.

No result. I attempt a step toward the people filing onto the ferry, but my legs refuse to move. These appendages know perfectly well that a ferry is a type of a boat... which will go *over water*.

I grit my teeth. This is something I tried not to think about on the way over, but now I have no choice. If I don't do something, Jane is going to go sailing—and I know that it's probably irrational, but I'm convinced that if I let her get on the ferry alone, I'll lose her... the way I lost my parents.

Or maybe it's not so irrational. When I was seven, I remember hearing about a Staten Island Ferry crash, where many people were killed and even more were injured.

No. I'm going to save Jane even if I have to swim after her.

I force myself to take a step toward the fucking ferry-boat. Then another. Then another.

Why am I moving so slowly? The boat will depart soon.

Straining my muscles and my sanity, I remind myself that there are people out there running into burning buildings and flying bullets while my dragon seems to be a docked boat.

The pep talk doesn't work particularly well. My breathing still speeds up with each step, and by the time I actually get onto the cursed boat, I sound like the bellows at a smithy.

Looking around frantically, I scare a few passengers but do not see Jane.

"Jane!" I shout croakily.

More people look at me askance, but I ignore them and shout her name again.

Behind me, undocking preparations begin, making my heart jackrabbit into my throat.

I'm too late. The ferry is about to leave, which means

Jane and I are about to share whatever dreadful fate awaits.

If only I could find her before—

"Adrian?"

My head snaps up.

Jane is staring down at me from the second floor of the boat. "What are you doing here?"

Yes! I found her. Sprinting around all the other passengers, I get to the second floor in one breath.

Grabbing Jane's wrist, I pull her to the ferry exit.

"What's going on?" she demands but allows me to keep dragging her. "Where are we going?"

"No time," I grit out and drag her to the first floor... which is when I see it.

We're already undocked and... are swimming.

No. Floating.

No. Moving.

Whatever you call it, this means it's officially too late. My legs jellify and I sink into a nearby chair. Jane sits next to me, her indignant expression turning into one of concern.

"Is it the water thing?" she asks me.

I manage a small nod. "I just need a second."

The boat begins to move in earnest. My stomach churns, and I start to feel dizzy and then promptly seasick.

Oh, yeah. I completely forgot that I get seasick on boats, even though it's the reason I wasn't with my parents the day they—

"Oh, my," Jane says when she spots my no-doubt

green expression. "Just relax," she croons and hugs me. "It's only a twenty-five-minute ride."

Twenty-five minutes? It feels like days of agony pass, and if I had state secrets that someone needed, I would spill them just to have the boat dock somewhere. Anywhere.

Since I have no secrets, I just suffer. But I do make a solemn vow to myself. If, by some miracle, we manage to survive this, I'm going to buy a pharmaceutical company and invent something much stronger than Dramamine for the unfortunate souls who don't have private jets and limos and therefore cannot avoid this horrific mode of transportation.

"We have to get off," Jane says, as if from the shore. "Or else we'll go back."

We've stopped? Finally. I stand on my wobbly legs and let Jane help me onto dry land, where I plop on a bench and do my best to catch my breath.

In mere minutes, I feel like a new man, which means very soon after that, I feel like an idiot over how I handled that whole situation.

I think it may be time I see a therapist and work on the swimming thing. If Jane were to fall in a lake or get on a cruise ship—

Jane grips my hand. "Are you okay?"

I turn to her, focusing on her gorgeous face and the concern in her amber eyes.

"Much better now," I say—and it's almost true. I'm over the boat ride, but being so close to Jane reawakens certain yearnings in Yoda.

"Want to get away from the water?" she asks.

I want to kiss her for that... or simply just kiss her. "Yes, please."

She still holds my hand as we rush to the first available cab, but I wince internally when Jane gives the driver her childhood home address. That destination implies she doesn't want to go back to my place —a place I had hoped she was beginning to see as ours.

Unless, does she think I'll lose my shit when we get to the Verrazzano Bridge, the way I did on the ferry?

She pushes her glasses up her nose—a gesture that should not be as sexy as it is. "Can you talk now?"

"Yeah," I say. "I'm completely fine."

Lie, that is. Calm, Yoda is not.

"Great," Jane says and grips my hand again. "I'm sorry that Sydney got a hold of the contract."

I open my mouth to reply, but she shushes me with a finger—making me wonder how insulting she'd find it if I licked it, or sucked on it, or—

"I'm also sorry that I ran away when they showed it on the screen," Jane continues. "It's just that, when I saw you look at me the way you did, I—"

"Stop," I say firmly, and her finger leaves my mouth. "I'm the one who is sorry. The only thing I can say in my defense is that I instantly realized you had nothing to do with that."

"But I did," she says. "I used a shitty password, and Sydney got—"

"No. Not your fault." I lay my other hand over her

small palm. "And it's moot anyway because I got custody of Piper despite the document."

She opens her mouth wide, which makes me want to kiss it more. "I didn't mess things up for you?"

"*Sydney* didn't mess things up for me," I correct. "But yes. No."

She narrows her eyes. "Then why didn't you tell me that right away? I've been kicking myself all this time."

"I tried calling you. And texting."

She pulls out her phone, glances at it, and grimaces. "I'm sorry. If I'd picked up, I would've spared you that horrible boat ride and myself some of the grief."

"Don't worry about it," I say. "But speaking of forgiveness, I want to apologize for something else."

Face going pale, Jane draws back. "Who you sleep with isn't any of my business."

I frown. "Who I sleep with?" And then it hits me. "I *told* you that wasn't what it looked like. Nothing happened between me and Sydney."

Jane sighs. "You don't owe me an explanation. Our marriage is fake and—"

"Nothing happened," I enunciate the words as firmly as I can. "Somehow, Sydney got into the building outside of the times designated for dropping off Piper. Then she got naked and woke me up in some last-ditch attempt at seduction, but I asked her to leave. Angry words were exchanged. That's it. I swear."

"Oh, wow." Then Jane's eyes widen. "I think she might've used my stupid password then as well."

"Ah. Right." I smile to take the sting out of my next

words as I add, "Maybe you *should* use different pass-words for things going forward."

She vigorously nods. "That's what I was doing on the cab ride to the ferry. Changing all my passwords."

I scoot over and look into her eyes. "Now that that's out of the way, what I actually want to apologize for are the things I said after our wedding night."

Her lips part. "What do you mean?"

I take her hand in mine. "I've hated acting like strangers for the last few weeks. I can't bear knowing that it's all my fault. I never should have—"

The car comes to a stop, and I realize we're next to Jane's house. But whose limo is that? Did I forget telling my driver to meet me?

Boat amnesia is definitely something to tell my future therapist about.

"Let's continue talking inside?" Jane gestures at her house.

I nod and pay the driver.

Getting out, I open the door for Jane, and just as she steps onto the pavement, I spot a big problem in our way.

Climbing out of the limo is Sydney.

Her eyes look puffy and her expression forlorn.

Fuck.

How bad of a father does she think I am that she needs to be so distraught?

Sydney takes a menacing step toward us, and her eyes aren't on me but on Jane. There's something really weird about the lingering stare, and I don't like it one bit. Between Sydney looking so unstable right now, and her showing up at my house naked last night, I would not be all that surprised if she pulled out a gun and shot Jane—and then demanded that I marry *her*.

Well, screw that. After surviving the ferry ride, this is nothing.

Putting myself between Sydney and Jane, I demand icily, "What are you doing here?"

CHAPTER 38

Jane

Before Adrian blocks my view, I get a chance to look at Sydney as if for the first time—and to realize just how much we look alike. That realization stirs all sorts of impossible-to-untangle emotions. The key one, strangely, is that I want to get to know this woman a little better, despite hating her guts so recently.

Unlike Tristan, who chose not to be in my life, Sydney had no choice, and it seems that in her own twisted way, she longs to have a family.

"I can't believe you just left after the hearing was done," Sydney sneers at Adrian. "Just as it was time to put together a visitation schedule that you claimed you so desperately wanted."

"I went after Jane," he snaps back. "Who was hurt by your stunt, I might add."

"Oh, please. We're not in court anymore, so you don't have to pretend that your little marriage is actually real."

That one hurts a lot because it's true.

Adrian's back tenses. "You're unbelievable. First, you—"

"Shut up," I say, snapping out of my paralysis. Stepping from behind Adrian so I can see Sydney's face, I clarify, "And I'm talking about the both of you. Seriously, you now share custody of a wonderful little human, so you need to learn how to act like adults, and soon."

Adrian looks like his sheepish dog, and to her credit, Sydney appears somewhat chastised as well.

"I didn't come here to fight," she says in a calmer tone, looking at me. "Or even to talk to him."

"Then why did you come?" Adrian demands again. "And how do you even know where Jane lives?"

"The background check, obviously," she replies with an eyeroll. Returning her attention to me, she says quietly, "Your mother said you went here after my dad's revelations."

Ah, so Tristan told her. Not great timing if you ask me. But then again, if he had great timing, he'd probably already be in my life.

"What does Tristan have to do with anything?" Adrian asks.

Crap. I never got a chance to tell him the big news.

Ignoring him, Sydney looks at me searchingly. "Do you think it's true?"

"Is what true?" Adrian asks.

"Stay out of this," Sydney snaps at him. More calmly, she adds, "Please. This is between me and Jane."

I put a reassuring hand on Adrian's shoulder. "Let us

talk. I'll explain shortly." To Sydney, I say, "I still haven't fully processed it myself, but I think it *is* true... especially when I look at you."

We stare at each other some more. I feel Adrian's shoulder tightening further under my hand, so before he can snipe at my sister some more, I blurt, "Tristan is the sperm donor. Sorry I didn't get a chance to tell you on our way over. I was going to—"

"He's what?" Adrian looks like his brain is about to explode.

"My father is her father," Sydney says to him snidely. "We're half-sisters. Don't you see how much she looks like me? You clearly have a type." She swings her gaze to me. "And I mean that last one as a compliment."

I guess if you think as highly of yourself as she does, stating that she and I are the same "type" *is* a compliment.

"What is she talking about?" says a small voice from behind me.

Oh, shit. I spin around and see Mary standing there with her backpack, eyes wide as two quarters.

Right. School is already out.

"Who is that?" Sydney asks, her own eyes widening.

"Why did she say she's your sister?" Mary demands.

Oh, crap. I guess there's no easing her into it.

"Mary, this is Sydney, Piper's mom," I say in a measured tone. I face Sydney. "This is my little sister, Mary. Like you and I, Mary and I share a parent... but it isn't Tristan."

Mary's eyes gleam with excitement, and in one single

breath she rattles out, "You learned who your father is? That's awesome. And he's Piper's mom's father too? That means you're Piper's aunt! Does that mean that I'm also Piper's aunt?"

I look at Sydney for help with that last one. Strictly speaking, Piper and Mary do not share any DNA, but I don't have the heart to explain that.

To my utter amazement, the corners of Sydney's lips lift and—speaking in babytalk for some unknown reason —she croons, "Of course, sweetie. You can be Piper's honorary aunt."

"Cool," Mary says. "But why are you talking to me like I'm a toddler? I'm ten years old."

"Going on forty," I add.

Sydney smiles in earnest now. In a normal voice, she says, "If you're Piper's honorary aunt, can I be your honorary sister?"

"Yes," Mary says without hesitation.

Sydney looks my way, her usual haughtiness tempered with uncertainty. "You're okay with that, right?"

I hesitate, then nod. Because what the hell? Whatever my newly discovered half-sister's issues are, she does seem to like kids and be good with them.

Or so I assume. If she were a bad mom to Piper, Adrian would've likely hired assassins instead of lawyers.

I decide to extend an olive branch too. "I'm okay with it if my mom is."

And poof—a black Cadillac pulls up to the curb at that moment, and Mom steps out.

Because of course.

"Wow," Mary says. "Speak of the devil, and she'll splurge on an Uber Black."

As Mom walks up to us, she doesn't seem to be surprised to see Sydney or Adrian here—or she's a good actress.

"Mom." Mary points at Sydney. "Can I be her honorary sister?" Looking sheepish, she turns to said honorary-sister-to-be and adds, "What was your name again?"

"Sydney. Like the city in Australia."

"Cool. I'm Mary, in case you forgot. After Marianne Dashwood, from *Sense and Sensibility*."

Mom shakes her head. "Mary is your grandmother's name."

"It is?" Mary cocks her head. "How did I not know that?"

"Because you only have the one," I theorize. "If there were two, you'd need to designate them, either by name or nickname."

"I'm pretty sure I've mentioned it," Mom says. "But let's get back to the honorary sister business." She turns to Sydney. "I'll consider it if you let me be Piper's honorary grandmother in return."

As Sydney examines my mom, she reminds me of Mrs. Corsica. "Can we get to know each other a little first?" she says after a long pause.

"I was just thinking the same thing," Mom says. "Want to come in for tea?"

Sydney nods and they all go into the house, leaving me and Adrian looking at each other in befuddlement.

Mrs. Westfield must applaud the choice of tea as the refreshment for any civilized tête-à-tête.

"Should we go somewhere else?" Adrian asks. "I still need to talk to you."

"How about my room?" I point up. I've always wanted to bring a hot guy there and have never got the chance.

Adrian smiles. "Will your mother mind?"

"No, but we shouldn't tell her, or else she'll provide us with condoms and unsolicited sex advice."

His expression turns roguish. "Want to sneak me into your room?"

I grin like a loon. "I thought you'd never ask."

And so, the two of us, grown-ass adults, tiptoe up the staircase and then to my room—even though the loud conversation in the kitchen makes the stealth unnecessary.

"Called it." Adrian points at all the bulging bookshelves. "Historical romance, right?"

"Yes, but that's not the only thing that defines me," I say with mock sternness. "I bet you didn't know about this." I pick up the stuffed penguin I used to sleep with... until *very* recently. "Mr. Tuxedo has no connection to those books whatsoever."

"I wouldn't dream of condensing you to just one thing," Adrian says. "Though if I did, it wouldn't be books. It would be your blushing cheeks."

Great. My treacherous cheeks choose that exact moment to turn red, as if to help him make his point.

"Yes, those." He leans in and pecks one of the burning cheeks with his cool, luscious lips. Drawing back to look at me, he says softly, "But I think I want to change my answer. If I had to define you by one thing, it would be your Mona Lisa-like smile. No. It would be how good you are with Piper. Actually, no. It would be—"

I grab his shoulders, rise on tiptoes, and lock lips with him, in part to shut him up but more so because I really, really want to.

He kisses me back fervently, but after a minute or so, he gently pulls away, even though heat still blazes in his eyes. His voice is rough. "Sorry, but I still need to tell you something."

I look at his lips longingly. "If it's about what you said after the wedding night, I forgive you. I think you were actually right. Piper is worth being careful. But now that the hearing has gone your way, maybe we can—"

Adrian cradles my face in his palms, scrambling my brain so much I forget how to speak.

I think I see what he's about to say in his eyes before his lips move, and then he utters three words: "I love you."

My heart turns into a bunny on steroids.

"It's something I realized at the hearing," he continues. "But I think I've felt it for a long time. I was just afraid to let myself—"

"I love you too," I say, coming out of my stupor. "I

love your roguish eyes, your rakish grin, your inventive-
ness. And—not to sound like a copycat—I love the way
you are with Piper. No. I love—"

This time, he's the one who kisses me, and we imbue
this kiss with all the things we haven't yet gotten the
chance to say to each other, like how I also hated it when
we didn't speak. Or how I dreamed of kissing him again,
and not just kissing but also—

As if reading my thoughts, Adrian begins to undress,
first himself and then me—all without stopping the kiss.

When we're naked, he whispers, "It shouldn't hurt
this time around."

And he's right. It doesn't.

It's like the best scene in every romance I've ever read,
only infinitely hotter because it's him.

The movie theater is brimming with VIPs, but all I care about is my husband sitting to my right. Yes, Adrian and I decided to stay married, so he *really* is my husband now, not just one in the eyes of the law.

He grasps my hand, and between that and the movie starting, my heartbeat skyrockets. Adrian has worked tirelessly on this project but has kept it a secret from me, all so I could enjoy this viewing tonight. All he's told me ahead of time is that I inspired him to do this, and that he thinks I might like it. Oh, and that he personally wrote the screenplay, composed the score, designed some of the costumes, and a whole laundry list of other accomplishments.

Put another way, I'm more amped than a kid after a tiramisu-eating contest.

I watch, enthralled, as the first scene unfolds. If Adrian's goal was to please viewers like me, he's totally nailed it.

The setting is England circa mid-1830s—one of my favorites—and there's a great love story in the film, making it a historical romance. The lovers in question are Ada Lovelace and Charles Babbage, real historical people, though the relationship is fictionalized. Charles was an eccentric genius inventor who—and this is hard-to-believe-but-true history—developed plans for a mechanical computer, a machine that, sadly, was never built (or else cat videos might've become a favorite pastime of humans a hundred years sooner). Ada was a talented mathematician and the only legitimate daughter of Lord Byron. Because she wrote programs for Charles's machine, she is now credited as the world's first computer programmer. That's right. She was the first in a field in which women today still hold only about thirty percent of the jobs, and she was in it at a time when women were considered incapable of learning mathematics with their feeble, tiny lady brains.

Needless to say, by the time credits roll, my eyes are teary. Leaping to my feet, I clap, and the rest of the audience joins in.

"You're a genius," I tell Adrian fervently.

He grins at me. "You really liked it?"

"Yeah," I say. "It's now my favorite movie."

Before he can reply, a reporter who introduces himself as a movie critic for *The New York Times* begins gushing to Adrian about how much he loved the film.

As soon as the reporter finishes, the mayor congratulates Adrian on a job well done, and then one of the actors stops by to thank Adrian for giving him a chance to be part of such an amazing project. Other people come by too, and it goes on for almost an hour.

When we get to the lobby, everyone we know is already waiting for us—the only person missing is Piper because bringing a toddler to a movie premiere is against the Geneva Conventions.

"That was actually watchable," says Bernard.

"For a movie without car chases and explosions," Michael corrects.

"Hey, it's the best sappy romance I've ever seen," Warren chimes in. "Not that I've seen all that many."

"You three are crazy," Mary says without ungluing her gaze from her phone. "The movie was the GOAT. Don't you think so, sis?"

The "sis" in question is Sydney—who's been getting along with Mary extremely well. It might have something to do with the fact that Mary has hit preteen-hood hard this past year and is drawn to Sydney's Queen Bee vibes. Mom and I are grateful to Sydney because she's thus far been able to talk Mary out of pink hair (what are you, an anime character?), a pierced nose (you'll look like a cow), and a tattoo of a dolphin (you're not enough of a tramp to get that stamp).

"You did a great job," Sydney says to Adrian with exaggerated graciousness.

"Thanks," Adrian replies, and I can tell he's doing his best to sound friendly—which is still a work in progress for these two. Hard work. But the fact that she's here today is evidence that she is trying.

On my end, I get along with my newfound half-sister pretty well considering she tried to sleep with my husband a mere year ago. It does help that she's started dating someone new, and that she's a good mom to Piper... and that she gets along with my own mom.

Hell, I think a few years from now, I might even like her.

"Great job?" Mom exclaims. "Understatement of the century! That was Oscar material."

"I agree," Tristan says. "Golden Globe too. That score was a work of high art."

I smile gratefully at the man I'm increasingly viewing less and less as the sperm donor. As with Sydney, the major reason I've warmed up to him is because of how much he adores Piper. He and I currently have a monthly brunch, and I'm thinking of upping that to biweekly, but I haven't told him that yet.

"I agree with all the praise," Mrs. Corsica chimes in. "And we will for sure stock this movie at the library when it is available."

She really means that *I* will stock it. She recently told me that she plans to retire, and that she will recommend me to be the one who takes her throne.

"Thank you all so much for coming out to support me," Adrian says. "I assume we'll see you at the afterparty?"

Once everyone answers in the affirmative, Adrian

grabs my wrist and drags me out of the theater, through the crowd of paparazzi, and into the limo.

As we pull off, he pours us both a glass of champagne, but I don't drink mine. Instead, I catch his gaze. "Your surprise is going to be hard to beat," I say, "but I will try."

Adrian eyes me curiously. "Is it a new outfit?"

I smile. "That too. I got something with lots of lace. I'll wear a chemise under it. But that's not comparable to the movie—even if tangentially related to the surprise."

"You like to tease a little too much," Adrian says.

It's true. I started off our sex life as a virgin, but with our twice and sometimes three times per day sexcapades, my skills in the bedroom now resemble those of an experienced courtesan, and teasing is par for the course.

Mrs. Westfield believes there's a line past which marital duty becomes wanton behavior. A line that, in this case, was crossed eleven months and three weeks ago.

"Fine," I say. "Spoilsport. Here's a hint: the surprise has to do with a certain IUD I recently took out."

Eyes widening, Adrian snatches the champagne glass from my hand, as though he thinks I might accidentally drink it. "You mean—"

"Indeed. I am with child." I've wanted to say that for ages. "Turns out, that movie isn't the only amazing thing you've created lately."

Grinning, Adrian sweeps me up into a warm hug, all the while telling me how exciting this is and how much he loves me. Finally letting me go, he says, "When everyone liked the movie, I didn't think today could go any better, but you've just improved on it, exponentially."

His words make me feel light and glowy. "Are you ready to write more children's stories?" I ask. "Or will you use the same ones, and just replace Piper's name and likeness with the those of your unborn baby?"

"I'll write new ones." He bends down and kisses my belly through my dress. "It will be a labor of love."

I press the button that closes the privacy partition of the limo—a not-so-subtle hint of where my mind is at.

Adrian's eyes grow hooded. "Here, now? What about the outfit?"

"That, dear husband, is hours away." I unbutton the collar of his shirt.

"Good point," he says and promptly rids me of my dress.

I kiss him then, a passionate, greedy kiss that makes promises of things to come.

Wonderful things.

Naughty things.

Exciting things.

And as he kisses me back, I taste his promise of our everlasting love.

Sneak Peeks

Thank you for participating in Jane and Adrian's journey!

Ready for more hot billionaires? Check out *Billionaire Grump*, a fake relationship romcom about a sharp-tongued aspiring botanist, a sexy, Ancient Rome-obsessed grump, and one fateful encounter in an elevator that goes hilariously wrong.

Need more adorable pets? Read *Puppy Love*! When Lilly lays eyes on Bruce Roxford, his super cute Chihuahua puppy is no longer the only one drooling. But she's armed with a strongly worded note, ready to tell off the man whose bank took her childhood home...until he offers her a job as his live-in dog nanny, that is.

To make sure you never miss a release, sign up for the newsletter at mishabell.com.

Turn the page to read previews from *Billionaire Grump* and *Puppy Love*!

Excerpt from Billionaire Grump

BY MISHA BELL

Juno

When I'm late for a job interview and get stuck on an elevator with an annoyingly sexy, Ancient Rome-obsessed grump, the last thing I expect is for him to be the billionaire owner of the building. I also don't expect to almost kill him... accidentally, of course.

Sure, I don't get the plant care position I applied for, but I do receive an interesting offer.

Lucius needs to trick the public (and his grandma) into thinking he's in a relationship, and I need tuition money to get my botany degree. Our arrangement is mutually beneficial—that is, until I start catching feelings.

If being a cactus lover has taught me anything, it's that if you get too close, there's a good chance you'll end up hurt.

Lucius

Post-elevator incident, I'm left with three things: my favorite water bottle full of pee, a life threatening allergic reaction, and paparazzi photos of my "girlfriend" and I that make my Gram the happiest woman alive.

Naturally, my next step is to blackmail—I mean, convince—this (admittedly cute) girl to pretend to date me. That way, my grandma stays happy, and as a bonus, I can keep the gold diggers at bay.

Unfortunately, my arch nemesis, a.k.a. biology, kicks in, and the whole "not getting physical" part of our agreement becomes increasingly hard to abide by. Worse yet, the longer I'm with Juno, the more my delicately crafted icy exterior melts away.

If I'm not careful, Juno will tear down my walls completely.

"Are you calling me stupid?" I snap. Anyone could have trouble with these damn buttons, not just a person with dyslexia.

He looks pointedly at the buttons. "Stupid is as stupid does."

I grind my teeth, painfully. "You're an asshole. And you've watched *Forrest Gump* one too many times."

His lips flatten. "That movie wasn't the origin of that saying. It's from Latin: *Stultus est sicut stultus facit.*"

I roll my eyes. "What kind of pretentious *stultus* quotes Latin?"

The steel in his eyes is so cold I bet my tongue would get stuck if I tried to lick his eyeball. "I don't know. Maybe the 'idiot' who happens to like everything related to Rome, including their numerals."

My jaw drops open. "You made this decision?" I wave toward the elevator buttons.

He nods.

Shit. He probably heard me earlier, which means I started the insults. In my defense, he did make an idiotic choice.

I exhale a frustrated breath. "If you're such an expert on Roman numerals, you could've told me which one to press."

He crosses his arms over his chest. "You didn't ask me."

My hackles rise again. "Ask you? You looked like you might bite my head off for just existing."

"That's because you delayed—"

The elevator jerks to a stop, and the lights around us dim.

We both stare at the doors.

They stay shut.

He turns to me and narrows his eyes accusingly. "What did you press now?"

"Me? How? I've been facing you. Unfortunately."

With an annoying headshake, he stalks toward the

panel with the buttons, and I have to leap away before I get trampled.

"You probably pressed something earlier," he mutters. "Why else would we be stuck?"

Why is it illegal to choke people? Just a few seconds with my hands on his throat would be a calming exercise.

Instead, I glare at his back, which is blocking my view of what he's doing, if anything. "The poor elevator probably just committed suicide over these Roman numerals. It knew that when someone sees things like L and XL, they think of T-shirt sizes for Neanderthal types like you. And don't get me started on that XXX button, which is a clear reference to porn. It creates a hostile work env—"

"Can you shut up so I can get us out of this?" he snaps.

His words bring home the reality of our situation: it's been over a minute, and the doors are still closed.

Dear saguaro, am I really stuck here? With this guy? What about my interview?

"Silence, finally," he says with satisfaction and moves to the side, so I see him jam his finger at the "help" button.

"It's a miracle that's not in Latin," I can't help but say. "Or Klingon."

"Hello?" he says into the speaker under the button, his voice dripping with irritation.

No reply, not even static.

"Anyone there?" His annoyance is clearly rising to new heights. "I'm late for an important meeting."

"And I'm late for an interview," I chime in, in case it matters.

He pauses to arch a thick eyebrow at me. "An interview? For what position?"

I stand straighter. "I'm sure the likes of you don't realize this, but the plants in this building don't take care of themselves."

Wait. Have I said too much? Could he torpedo my interview—assuming this elevator snafu hasn't done it already? What does he do here, anyway—design ridiculous elevators? That can't be a full-time job, can it?

"A tree hugger," he mutters under his breath. "That tracks."

What an asshole. I've never hugged a tree in my life. I'm too busy talking to them.

He returns his scowling attention to the "help" button—though now I'm thinking it should've been labeled as "no help."

"Hello? Can you hear me?" he shouts. "Answer now, or you're fired."

I roll my eyes. "Is it a good idea to be a dick to the person who can save us?"

He blows out an audible breath. "It doesn't matter. The button must be malfunctioning. They wouldn't dare ignore me."

I pull out my trusty phone, a nice and simple Nokia 3310. "Full of yourself much?"

He stares at my hands incredulously. "So that's why the elevator got stuck. It went through a time warp and transported us to 2008."

I frown at the lack of reception on my Nokia. "This version was released in 2017."

"It still looks dumber than a brain-dead crash test dummy." He proudly pulls an iPhone from his pocket. "*This* is what a phone should look like."

I scoff. "That's what constant distraction looks like. Anyway, if your iNotSoSmartPhone—trademarked—is so great, it should have some reception, right?"

He glances at his screen, but I can tell he already knows the truth: no reception for his darling either.

Still, I can't resist. "See? Your genius of a phone is just as useless. All it's good for is turning people into social-media-checking zombies."

He hides the device, like a protective parent. "On top of all your endearing qualities, you're a technophobe too?"

I debate throwing my Nokia at his head but decide it's not worth shelling out sixty-five bucks for a replacement. "Just because I don't want to be distracted doesn't mean I'm a technophobe."

"Actually, my phone is great at blocking out distractions." He puts the headphones back over his ears. "See?" He presses play, and I hear the faint riffs of heavy metal.

"Very mature," I mouth at him.

"Sorry," he says overly loudly. "I can't hear any distractions."

Fine. Whatever. At least he has good taste in music. My cactus and I are big fans of Metallica, which is what I think he's listening to.

I begin to pace back and forth.

I'm stuck, and I'm late. If this elevator jam doesn't resolve itself in the next minute or two, I can pretty much kiss the new job goodbye—and by extension, my tuition money. No tuition money means no botany degree, which has been my dream for the last few years.

By saguaro's juices, this sucks really bad.

I sneak a glance at the hottie—I mean, asshole.

What would he say about someone with dyslexia wanting a college degree? Probably that I'd need a university that uses coloring books. In truth, even coloring books wouldn't help that much—I can never stay inside those stupid lines.

I sigh and look away, increasingly worried. My dreams aside, what if the elevator stays stuck for a while?

The most immediate problem is my growing need to pee—but paradoxically, a longer-term worry will be finding liquids to drink.

I wonder... If you're thirsty enough, does your body reabsorb the water from the bladder? Also, could I MacGyver a filter to reclaim the water in my urine with what I have on me? Maybe through cat hair?

I shiver, and only partially from the insane AC that's somehow reaching me even in here. In the short term, it would be so much better if it were hot instead of cold. I'd sweat out the liquids and not need to pee, though I guess I'd die of thirst sooner. I sneak an envious glance at the large stranger. I bet he has a bladder the size of a blimp. He also has a stainless-steel bottle that's probably filled with water that he likely won't share.

There's also the question of food. I don't have

anything edible with me, apart from a can of cat food...
and, theoretically, the cat herself.

No. I'd sooner eat this stranger than poor Atonic.

As if psychic, the stranger's stomach growls.

Crap. With this guy being so big and mean, he'd
probably eat the cat. After that, he'd eat me... and not in
a fun way.

I'm so, so screwed.

Visit <u>www.mishabell.com</u> to order your copy of
Billionaire Grump today!

Excerpt from Puppy Love

BY MISHA BELL

Lilly

An opportunity to tell off the billionaire whose bank took my childhood home? Yes, please! The greedy, arrogant jerk thinks I'm here to interview for the job of his dog trainer (a.k.a. nanny), but he's got a big storm coming.

So what if Bruce Roxford is tall, muscular, and handsome? Nothing will stop me from giving him a piece of my mind—not even his adorable Chihuahua puppy, the insane amount of money he's offering for the gig, or his gorgeous, deep blue eyes...

The combination, though? I'm in trouble.

Bruce

Lilly Johnson is five minutes late for our scheduled interview, and I have never hired a tardy employee. But before I can send her away, my Chihuahua puppy falls in love with her.

Yes, just the Chihuahua.

This woman is unprofessional, difficult, snarky... and for some reason, impossible to get off my mind.

So, of course, I hire her as my live-in dog trainer. How bad of an idea could that be?

How the hell is he hot? Everything about Bruce Roxford is ice cold, from his arctic blue eyes to the frosty frown on his lips. Even his dark, sleeked-back hair has a cool, blue-black sheen to it instead of the usual warm brown undertones.

"Yes?" he demands, pointedly not opening his front door any wider.

Why is he acting like his security people didn't announce who I was? Not to mention, we have an appointment—and it's not like there are random people coming and going from his massive estate.

Doing my best not to shiver from the chill he exudes, I say, "I'm Lilly Johnson."

No reply.

"The dog trainer."

Silence.

"I'm here for an interview with Bruce Roxford?"

What I don't say is that the interview is just a pretext to give the heartless bastard a tongue lashing. His bank took my childhood home, so when I saw his ad looking for someone in my field, I knew it was fate.

Maybe I should just cuss him out now?

No. He'd slam the door in my face and have his security escort me off the premises. I need to have him as a captive audience. Before seeing him in person, I figured I'd lock us in a room and read the note that I've carefully composed for the occasion. That way, I wouldn't forget any insults or accusations. However, now that I'm face to face with this huge, broad-shouldered male specimen, I'm less sure about being alone with him, especially in a hostile situation.

He folds his muscular arm in front of his face and frowns at his A. Lange & Sohne watch. "You're late. Goodbye."

The words hit me like shards of hail.

"Late by five minutes," I retort, proud of how steady my voice is. "There was traffic and—"

"Traffic is as predictable a fact of life as taxes." He starts to close the door in my face.

I suck in a big breath. No time to read my whole spiel. A quick version will have to suffice.

Before I can let loose any vitriol, a blur of black fluff darts out from the tiny sliver between the door and its frame.

A guinea pig?

No. It's wagging its tail and licking my shoes.

Oh, right. It's a puppy—which makes sense given the ad.

My heart leaps. This is a long-haired Chihuahua—and a gorgeous one at that, with a silky pitch-black coat, white fur on its chest, a face that reminds me of a tiny bear, and brown patches above its eyes that look like curious eyebrows. Better yet, the lack of yappiness and ankle biting thus far makes me think this might be the friendliest member of this particular breed.

I crouch and pet its heavenly fur. "Hi there. Who are you?"

The puppy flops over, revealing that he's a good *boy*, as opposed to girl.

A bittersweet ache squeezes my chest as I scratch the little bald patch on his belly. It's been five years since I lost Roach, the canine love of my life, and he too was a Chihuahua—just much bigger, less friendly to strangers, and with a smooth coat.

To this day, whenever I come across a new member of this breed, a touch of sadness tarnishes the joy of meeting a dog. Luckily, because they are small, few people formally train Chihuahuas, so I've never had to pass on a client because of this. In any case, the joy quickly wins out as I move my fingers to scratch the puppy's fluffy chest, and he starts to look like he's mainlining heroin.

"You like that, don't you, sweetheart?" I croon.

As usual, my imagination provides me with the dog's response—which, for some unknown reason, is spoken in the impossibly deep voice of James Earl Jones, a.k.a. Darth Vader:

Do I like belly rubs? That's like asking if I like howling at the moon. Or licking my balls. Or eating a—

Somewhere far above me, I hear someone blow out an exasperated breath.

Oh, shit. I forgot where I am. It's a common occurrence when dogs are involved.

Straightening to my full height (which, admittedly, is barely five feet), I stare up challengingly into my nemesis's blue eyes—which look wider now, like fishing holes in an icy lake.

"How did you do that?" he demands.

I nervously tuck a strand of hair behind my ear. "Do what?"

He gestures at the tail-wagging Chihuahua. "Colossus is never friendly. With anyone."

So maybe he *is* typical for his breed. I grin, unable to help myself. "Colossus? What is he, like two pounds?"

"Two and a half," he says, expression still stern. "Do you have bacon in your pockets?"

Feeling like I'm on trial, I pull out my pockets to show they're empty. "I never feed dogs bacon. Even the safest kinds have too much fat and sodium, not to mention other flavorings that—"

"Okay," he interrupts imperiously.

I blink at him. "Okay what?"

"You've got the job."

∽

Visit www.mishabell.com to order your copy of *Puppy Love* today!

Made in the USA
Middletown, DE
15 October 2023